The claustrophobic space gave her the creeps.

Meg walked slowly through the bowels of the ferry's empty parking deck, as dark and silent as catacombs. The sight of it tightened the knot of nerves in her chest. And reminded her just how terrified she'd been above deck not a couple of hours ago.

She got in her car, eager to meet Jack and head over to the police station. As jittery as she was, she locked the doors.

She refused to believe that the attack on the ferry had been anything other than random—brutal, terrifying, life-shaking—and yet not the slightest bit personal. She wouldn't let a killer steal away the peace in her soul.

As she eased the car down the ramp, something rustled behind her seat. Shopping bags fell over, spilling their contents. A dark shadow rose to fill the rearview mirror.

She looked up, and into the deep, menacing hood of an orange raincoat. Could it be? The Raincoat Killer was real...and here for her....

Books by Maggie K. Black

Love Inspired Suspense

Killer Assignment
Deadline

MAGGIE K. BLACK

is an award-winning journalist and romantic suspense author. Her writing career has taken her around the globe, and into the lives of countless grassroots heroes and heroines, who are faithfully changing lives and serving others in their own communities. Whether flying in an ultralight over the plains of Africa, riding a camel past the pyramids in Egypt or walking along the Seine in Paris, Maggie finds herself drawn time and again to the everyday people behind her adventures, and seeing how we are all touched by the same issues of faith, family and community.

She has lived in the American South and Midwest, as well as overseas. She currently makes her home in Canada, where her husband teaches history at a local high school. After walking her two beautiful princesses to school, she either curls up on the couch to write, with the help of her small but mighty dog, or heads to her local coffee shop. She is thankful to her readers for allowing her to turn the adventures, and people who have inspired her, into fresh stories that made her pulse race and her heart soar.

DEADLINE
MAGGIE K. BLACK

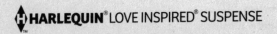

HARLEQUIN® LOVE INSPIRED® SUSPENSE

™ LOVE INSPIRED BOOKS

ISBN-13: 978-0-373-67626-2

DEADLINE

www.Harlequin.com

Printed in U.S.A.

There is no fear in love.
But perfect love drives out fear.
—*1 John* 4:18

With thanks to Keren.
My life is less stormy because of you.

ONE

Deep gray fog rolled over the surface of Lake Huron, slipping through the open door to the ferry deck, and blocking out the afternoon sun. Meg Duff braced her palm against the doorframe and took in a long, cleansing breath. The smell of impending rain filled the air. She stood with her feet just inside the threshold of the crowded passenger lounge. Pale blue eyes stared out into the void. Wind brushed against her face, tossing her dark, chin-length hair. A shiver ran down her spine. The deck was deserted.

Just two more days until the wedding, Meg. All you've got to do is hold it together until then. Somewhere on this boat were a young bride and groom headed to Manitoulin Island for their dream wedding. The last thing they needed was to find out their wedding planner was having a panic attack.

She glanced at her cell phone. Twenty minutes until they reached shore. Her palm pressed against her chest. She focused on its rhythmic rise and fall. As the only professional wedding planner on a beautiful and remote island, she'd organized more than her fair share of weddings for big-city couples, who'd parachute into her community just long enough say "I do" and cut the cake. But this wedding had quickly become the most expensive and demanding of her career. The young couple were college students in Toronto, who'd agreed to get married on the island to butter up the bride's elderly grandmother who lived there, and who was paying the bills. The wedding had been organized solely with the high-strung bride, and almost entirely by phone and email. Within five minutes of joining the wedding party at the mainland ferry docks, the bride had launched into a string of ridiculously detailed questions about decorations at the reception venue, while the imposing best man had made an unwanted romantic advance that left Meg feeling both flustered and insulted.

But that was nothing compared to the panic that had coursed through her when she looked into the young groom's eyes and was struck by flashbacks of a tragic night so many years ago.

Why hadn't she realized she was actually planning a wedding for the cousin of someone whose senseless death still haunted her nightmares?

It had been fourteen years since a truck had collided with two teenaged boys on snowmobiles—

the groom's cousin Chris, and Meg's younger brother, Benji. She'd been seventeen. But the young groom, Wesley, had only been seven at the time. His family had moved off the island shortly afterward. She hadn't even recognized his name until she'd seen his face. He'd given no sign that he recognized hers. Did the groom and his bride even know how that night also tore her life in two? Should she tell them? Surely if she didn't, someone else on the island would. But how could she damper the happiest day of their lives by bringing up memories like that?

A bag knocked hard against her back, almost forcing her out into the fog. She glanced over her shoulder, but the culprit had already disappeared into the crowd without so much as an apology. She turned back to the gloom, shoved her phone into her pocket and wrapped her scarf twice around her neck. Crocheted strands tumbled down her slender frame, all the way to her knees, but did little to protect against the damp. Silhouettes of the shoreline swirled into focus for a moment, before being swallowed back up by the never-ending gray. She should really close the door.

"Excuse me, miss?"

There was a man behind her. Tall, with the broad shoulders and the tapered build of an athlete. His brown leather jacket was faded and worn, while his tousled, sun-kissed hair would've made her presume he was just another thrill-seeking tourist if it wasn't for how very intently his dark eyes were now searching her face.

A flush of heat rose to her cheeks. "Can I help you?"

His mouth turned up ever so slightly into a casual, laid-back grin. But the intensity of his gaze never faltered for a second. The warmth spread down her neck and through her shoulders. It looked like the smile of a man who'd seen more than his fair share of danger.

It was the kind of smile that made her feel anything but safe.

"My name is Jack Brooks. I'm a reporter with *Torchlight News,* Toronto." Too late she saw the voice recorder in his outstretched hand. He raised the microphone toward her. "Would it be all right if I asked you a few questions?"

Her blood ran cold. A *reporter?* Was the press actually going to cover this wedding? As if it wasn't bad enough she'd had to watch those scandal-seeking newshounds trampling all over her lawn as a teenager, while her brother lay in the hospital fighting for his life. They'd kept coming back, every few years, to revisit the story. Now it seemed she had to face them again, just because she hadn't been quick enough to realize a connection between that tragedy and this groom. Was the shadow of that night going to follow her for the rest of her life?

All this and it was still only Thursday. How was she ever going to make it through this weekend without falling apart?

Jack Brooks could waste all the handsome grins on her that he wanted. She knew the look of a man who was after something. He wasn't going to get it from her. "No. I'm sorry. I don't talk to reporters."

Then before he could say anything more, she pushed through the open doorway and out into the cool, damp air, barely even noticing something clatter behind her. He didn't follow. A thick blanket of gray enveloped her body. She strode down the deck. The babble of voices faded completely. Then the light of the lounge disappeared in the fog.

There was muffled sound to her right. A rustling, like footsteps shuffling. Hang on, had someone else actually wandered out on deck in this weather?

Meg turned. "Hello?" No one there. Silence filled her ears, except for the thrum of the engines beneath her. A jittery feeling brushed along the back of her neck. She slid her hands onto the railing.

Enough of this. She was stressed. Rattled. Nothing more. She just needed to pray. A deep breath filled her lungs. She let it out slowly. Her eyes closed as the words of her favorite hymn moved through her mind like a prayer, "Whatever my lot, Thou has taught me to say, It is well. It is well with my—"

The full-body blow was hard and without warning as her attacker pushed her into the railing. The air was knocked from her chest. A scream barely escaped from her lungs before a leather-gloved hand clamped over her mouth, forcing her silent.

Ice-cold panic gripped her chest so tightly her body felt paralyzed. The attacker's other hand grabbed the scarf at her throat and twisted it like a noose. Slowly he squeezed the air from her windpipe. The desperate need to breathe burst through her body. She shoved back against her attacker with every ounce of energy she had. Her head thrashed. The gloved hand slipped just enough to let her glance back. But all she could see was the orange hood of a raincoat.

He shoved her forward again, pinning her body against the railing, her small frame no match for his strength. Then he let go of her mouth. She opened her lips, but could barely make a sound as she gasped to fill her lungs with air. He grabbed hold of the bottom ends of her scarf and twisted them around her wrists, tying her hands together. Then he lifted her off the deck. She kicked out hard, her feet desperately searching for grip while she wrenched her bound hands, trying to get them free. But even as she struggled, he forced her over the railing toward the unforgiving water below.

Jack leaned back against the door and pulled a page of crime pictures from his jacket. His eyes scanned the images: a ransacked college dorm room, a garbage-strewn alley and a trashed apartment. Places where three different young women were killed. The only connection anyone had been able to find was security camera footage and witness statements that described someone in an orange raincoat at each of the crime scenes.

Oh, Lord, why am I the only one who believes this is the work of a serial killer? He was risking his entire professional career on a hunch. Monday afternoon, he'd finally talked his editor at *Torchlight News* into running the article he'd cobbled together laying out his investigation thus far on the "Raincoat Killer." The story ran on the front cover of Tuesday's paper, and on Wednesday morning the chief of police himself had called a press conference to announce the murders were unrelated and that Jack's article was nothing but the product of an amateur sleuth jumping to ridiculous conclusions. His editor had suggested Jack take the rest of the week off while the publisher figured out whether or not to fire him.

Jack had decided instead to chase one final lead all the way up to Manitoulin Island. Either he'd find the proof his story was solid or face the fact that when he walked back into the office it would be to kiss his job goodbye. Every well-honed instinct in his journalistic gut was convinced these three murders were somehow connected. Especially now that he'd looked across a ferry and locked eyes on *her*.

His eyes zeroed in on a picture of the final crime scene. There, amid the broken glass and chaos, two flyers lay on the floor, next to where a young woman had been stabbed. One was an island ferry schedule, with this afternoon circled. The other read Meg Duff, Island Weddings above the picture of a beautiful woman with troubled blue eyes. The very same woman who'd just disappeared off into the fog.

A heavyset man jostled past him, his coffee slopping over the rim of his cup and onto the page. Jack leapt back and tripped over something. A cell phone. Was it Meg's? Had she dropped it in her hurry to get away from him? He slipped the phone and the wet pages into his bag. Well, she might not want to talk to him as a journalist, but he wouldn't be much of a gentleman if he didn't at least try to return her phone.

Jack shoved the door back open and walked outside. *Wow. It's like soup out here.* He strode down the deck, choosing a direction at random.

A scream split the air. Female. Terrified. He

started running. Then he saw them. A figure in a raincoat had wrestled Meg over the railing. Her hands were tied. Her feet kicked frantically. Adrenaline surged through Jack's body, pushing his legs into a flat-out sprint.

Meg's attacker threw her overboard.

TWO

Screams filled Jack's ears as Meg's body disappeared. The man in the raincoat turned. Was he face-to-face with the Raincoat Killer? The thought hit Jack like a punch to the gut. His eyes searched the hooded form for some clue to his identity. But he barely had seconds to look before the killer took off running.

Jack gritted his teeth. How long would it take him to find a member of the crew and tell him to sound the overboard alarm? Minutes. He'd learned that from covering too many drownings. Then even more precious minutes would pass as they stopped the ferry, lowered the lifeboat and went back to search the foggy water for the woman now fighting for her life. How long would it take them to find her? Could she even hold on that long? Was he willing to risk it?

No.

His bag hit the deck. Jack tossed off his leather jacket, grabbed a life ring from the railing and clutched it to his chest. *Dear Lord, please give me the strength to save her.* He leapt overboard. Air rushed past him. Choppy water hit Jack's body like a tidal wave, knocking the ring from his hands and throwing his sense of direction into chaos. The ring's towrope unraveled in the water around him. Identical walls of gray filled his vision on all sides. If he wasn't careful, he'd end up swimming in circles until both he and Meg drowned. "Hey! Hello! Shout if you can hear me!"

No answer but the rumble of the ferry departing in the distance. For a fraction of a second he closed his eyes and focused on the fading sound of the engine. Then he tied the end of the towrope to his belt and took off swimming in the opposite direction, dragging the ring behind him. "Hang on! I'm coming!"

Oh, Lord, please let her still be alive. Help me reach her in time.

"Help!" Her frightened voice pierced the gloom. "I'm—" The sound was swallowed up by the gurgle of water filling her throat.

"Hold on! I'm here!" *Please, Lord, please, help her hold on.* "I'm coming for you." His long limbs tore through the water. The fog parted and he saw her, breaking through the surface, thrashing against her bonds. Her eyes met his. Terrified. Exhausted. Water swept over her head again. She disappeared under the surface.

He dove for her. His eyes peered blind through the cold, dark depths. He found her, churning the water as she kicked frantically toward the surface. Her foot made contact with his knee. His leg went numb. He gasped and nearly swallowed a mouthful of water. If she didn't calm down enough to let him save her, neither of them would make it out alive.

His left arm slid around her waist. He pulled her against him. His right hand grabbed her bound wrists and slid them over his head. To his relief, her body fell still against his chest. Now he just had to be strong enough to swim for both of them.

His lungs burned with the urge to breathe. His heart pounded through his skull. The cold seeped through his clothes as his legs battled against the weight of his boots. But the rope tied to his waist kept him tethered to the life ring above. They burst through to the surface. He spluttered, then gasped for breath. She coughed hard; her body shuddered against his. Her head fell onto his shoulder, and he impulsively turned his face toward it, feeling her forehead brush against his chin. Her legs started treading water. *Thank God. Just. Thank. You. God.*

He pulled the life ring over. "I need you to let go of me so I can untie your hands. Okay?"

She nodded as shallow gasps slipped between

her lips. Carefully he slid her arms off his neck, pushed the life ring between them, and helped her lean her weight on it. They floated there for a moment, panting for breath, resting on opposite sides of the ring, their hands linked over the center. Tendrils of dark hair framed her face. Blue eyes looked up into his. Fragile and brave.

Questions poured through his brain. Was this some sick coincidence, or had he actually just saved this woman from the very serial killer that the Toronto police said didn't exist? Was there a personal connection between her and either the killer or the most recent victim, as he'd theorized from the crime photos? Did she even know about the murder of three young women, miles away in Toronto?

But even as the thoughts filled his mind, he could feel the hard-bitten journalist inside him battling against the unexpected desire to simply to reach up and cup her cheek in his hand, to comfort and reassure her.

Instead he reached for the twisted and torn fabric that still tied her wrists together. Judging by the state of it, she hadn't been about to give in without a fight.

"Thank you. You saved my life."

A grin of relief broke over his face. "No problem. I'm just thankful you were able to keep afloat long enough for me to reach you."

"I don't…" She shivered. "I don't know what just happened…or who that was…or why he'd… One moment I was standing on the deck. The next…" Her voice trailed off as her bound hands rose back toward the bruises now forming in the curve of her neck.

A seemingly random attack. By a man in an orange raincoat. This one right before his very eyes. And here he was, floating in the water, miles away from any way to make notes or to contact the police and his editor.

"It's okay. You're safe now. I promise." He gently pulled her hands back toward him.

She glanced toward the sound of the departing ferry. He could read the question in her eyes. *But what about everyone else still on the boat?* He wished he had an answer.

"My name is Meg Duff, by the way. But I'm guessing you already knew that."

So she'd suspected earlier that he'd sought her out specifically and that his questions for her weren't going to be just a random survey of public opinion. Again, questions about the Raincoat Killer filled his mind, but the last thing he wanted to do was frighten her any more than she already was. "You're a wedding planner, right? I saw a flyer of yours back in Toronto."

"I gave out hundreds at a bridal show there just

a few months ago. I'm guessing you already know all about the wedding this weekend."

He kept his face carefully blank. No, he didn't know. Weddings, parties and frilly dresses weren't the kinds of thing he'd ever covered. Not unless they were covered in blood and surrounded by crime tape.

"I'd gone to the mainland today to meet the bride for a dress fitting," she went on. "Then the rest of the wedding party arrived from Toronto. I was on the boat to escort them all to the island. But then I decided to step away onto the deck for a while to find some peace. They're a bit much."

He gently worked his fingers in between the strings and her wrists.

"It stretched," she added.

"What?"

"The fabric. Cotton does that." She breathed in deeply. "I thank God it was yarn, not silk, or I'd be dead by now."

Huh. She'd been attacked, nearly drowned, was now floating in a lake and yet she still had the ability to find something to be thankful for. He separated the loosest loop and yanked with all his might. It snapped. Gently he eased the fabric away from her wrists. His heart ached to see the deep red welts standing out on her pale skin. Then he unbound her neck. "Are you going to be okay to swim for shore?"

"Shouldn't we wait for the ferry to find us?"

He shook his head. "It's not coming back, unless someone else saw something and notified the captain. I didn't time have to alert the crew. It was either find help or save you. Last summer, a college kid jumped off a ferry like this and it took them almost fifteen minutes to reach him with a lifeboat, and that was with fifty witnesses pointing their phones at him." He'd covered the story. The kid had very nearly drowned. "Average ferry rescue time on a good day is twelve minutes. I saw that your hands were tied, and knew you'd need help faster than that."

Was that more information than she'd needed? He was overexplaining. A telltale sign he was nervous. How many years had it been since *that* had happened? But something about sharing a life ring in the cold gray water with this beautiful, frightened creature was setting his nerves on edge, and it wasn't only the hunch he'd just confronted a serial killer.

Keep your emotions out of it, Jack. You know you can't afford to get emotionally connected to anyone you intend to interview. Now even more than ever.

"Do you think anyone from the wedding party will come looking for you?"

"Not until after they land. I told them I'd meet

up with them when we docked on the island. Were you traveling with anyone?"

He shook his head. "I'm up here alone. So chances are no one even knows we've gone overboard."

"Except..." Her voice faltered.

"Except the criminal who did this to you."

A light rain began to fall, cooling the air and lightening the fog. "I'm ready to start swimming if you are," she said. "I have a pretty good guess of where we are, and it shouldn't take too long."

She swam with one hand, keeping the other braced on the life ring. He did likewise.

"Do you cover a lot of weddings?"

"No. Never. I'm a crime reporter."

She frowned. The same uncertainty he'd seen in her face, when she'd brushed him off before, filled her eyes. She'd probably run from him again if she had anywhere to go.

"I'm sorry if I seemed rude earlier," she said, "I thought you wanted to interview me about the wedding I'm organizing this weekend. But now I'm realizing that probably wasn't it."

He nearly laughed. "Is the couple rich or famous?"

Another pause, filled with nothing but the sound of their bodies cutting through the water.

"Not really," she said. "Just young and immature. The bride's grandmother owns a big chunk of the island, so the wedding is pretty lavish. The bride lost her parents when she was young and was raised by her grandmother. The bride and groom have both seen far more than their fair share of tragedy actually, which might be why they decided to get married so young. The groom's parents died just last year, and his cousin was in a bad snowmobile accident years ago." She glanced at him sideways. "In my experience, reporters like poking around in human misery."

There was a bitter edge to her voice, as though she'd been hurt before and was still cradling the wound.

"Trust me, I'm not that kind of reporter."

"So, what did you want to ask me about?"

The distant shoreline appeared and disappeared in a haze of rolling fog. The rain grew heavier. *Lord, help me find the right words.* It was hard to imagine a worse time for this conversation. But he also had no idea what was going to happen when they got to shore, and she deserved to hear it from him first, before they reported the attack to the police. He took a deep breath. "Have you ever heard of Krista Hooper, Eliza Penn or Shelly Day?"

"No. Are they brides?"

"They're murder victims."

Her face paled. "I don't understand."

He kept his voice steady, focusing on the facts, not theories. "All three died recently in Toronto.

In each case, there is evidence suggesting that the killer was wearing an orange raincoat."

She stopped swimming so abruptly he accidentally yanked the life ring from her hands. "You're saying there's a serial killer on the loose? Is he the one who tried to drown me?"

He pushed the floatation device toward her. She didn't grab it. "I'm saying I honestly don't know. A couple of days ago, my paper, *Torchlight News,* ran a full, front-page article by me that argued we were dealing with a serial killer. I thought it was solid. But the chief of police held a press conference yesterday and announced investigators are still confident they're just three unrelated attacks." Not to mention the chief had then denounced his article as fear mongering, almost destroying Jack's career and reputation in a fatal blow.

Meg treaded water. "But three young women were murdered?"

"In a city of millions." He could feel a bite slipping into his voice. Oh yes, he knew the arguments against his story far too well. "Three young women dying within the space of a three months is rare, but not unheard of."

"But what about the orange raincoat?"

"It could have come from any hardware store. It could just be a coincidence that there happened to be a bystander wearing a similar raincoat in each case. Even if the killer really was wearing a raincoat, some are suggesting whoever killed Eliza Penn and Shelly Day might have seen my first news story on Krista Hooper, so he grabbed his own coat as a copycat disguise." Yeah, as if it wasn't bad enough he'd been called a shoddy journalist, he was actually being accused of giving criminals ideas on how to get away with murder. "Also, all three victims died in different ways. The first was hit over the head during a burglary gone bad. The second was struck by a car. And the third was stabbed. The final victim, Shelly, had a flyer for your wedding services in her apartment, and island ferry schedules turned up somewhere near each crime scene. So I'd just wanted to ask if you knew them."

"Not as far as I know." Meg reached for the life ring. "I'll look up their names when I get home. One might have emailed about booking a wedding. But I give out thousands of flyers each year. You could have just called me."

Right, except his editor wanted him out of the office until the storm died down, and every instinct in his gut was convinced the fact that the last island ferry schedule had this afternoon clearly circled was no coincidence.

"What do you call him?" she asked. "This killer?"

"In my article, I called him the Raincoat Killer.

But again, the police will probably tell you something very different."

"What if you're right, though?" Her lips quivered. "What if we just left a serial killer on a ferry full of people? What if someone else was killed because you saved my life?"

He took her hands. "Listen. Don't do this. I've met way too many victims who drive themselves crazy thinking that somehow their survival came at the expense of someone else's. I was praying pretty hard when that monster threw you overboard—"

"Me too."

He smiled. "Then trust God that this was how our prayers got answered, and don't try to do the guesswork yourself." That's what he had to believe. Otherwise the lack of justice in the world would have destroyed him long ago.

They swam in silence for a few moments. He glanced at her face. Okay, he had to tell her something. Just enough to let her sleep at night. "If this even is the work of a serial killer, you should know that most serial killers have a type. In this case, he only goes after young, very beautiful, female targets and only when they are completely alone and isolated. He's been very smart when it comes to avoiding any potential witnesses."

Considering how close he himself had come to not venturing out on deck, the killer had almost pulled off the perfect crime yet again. Jack was stunned by the strength and determination it must have taken Meg to fight for her life long enough for him to reach her.

"Now," he said, "there are over six hundred people on that ferry right now. All of whom are probably crammed into the interior cabins like sardines waiting for the ferry to dock any minute now. So, even if I am right, the chance of him finding another attractive, solitary, female victim in that crowd, and then killing her without anyone seeing anything, is so close to unlikely that it's borderline impossible. And why would he be looking for anyone else? If he came on the ferry to commit a murder, then he probably thinks he succeeded. For all he knows, we're both dead."

It was likely the killer had slipped his disguise back into his bag and was now mingling with an unsuspecting public. Was the killer now standing, sullen in a corner, watching the crowd? Lurking in a hallway? Blending in with the crew? Or was he still on deck, staring back toward where he'd just thrown Meg's bound and helpless body?

It didn't matter what the chief of police, Jack's boss or the naysayers believed. Everything in his gut told him the gentle fingers now brushing against his had just fought back against a ruthless, relentless serial killer.

If only he'd been wrong.

THREE

Meg's bare feet brushed against a sheet of rock. Slippery but comforting nonetheless. She stumbled up shore, half walking and half climbing, until rock gave way to dirt. *Thank You, God.* When her body had first hit the water, she thought she'd never feel solid ground again. Nausea swept over her at the memory of the attacker's hand around her throat. Her head swung down between her knees. Jack's fingers brushed against the inside of her arm, pressing lightly against her skin. "You okay?"

She stared down at long legs, ending in sturdy brown boots with double-knotted laces. No wonder he hadn't kicked them off. She didn't even know when in the struggle she'd lost her shoes. His hand reached for hers. A strong hand, without any sign of a wedding band. She let him help her up onto the shore. "I'm fine. Thank you."

She turned toward him, coming face-to-face with the wet black T-shirt stretched tightly across his chest. His dark, unflinching eyes seemed to stare right into hers as if she were a mystery he was intent on solving. There was something about him that made her feel both small and protected at the same time. It was unnerving.

And for some reason she was still holding his hand. "Thank you. Again. For everything." She let go and started walking quickly up the bank toward the harbor, hoping he wouldn't notice the flush that had risen to her cheeks.

The rain had stopped and the fog had cleared, but a general damp still hung in the air. They'd drifted into the woods not far from where the ferry docked. Yet another reason to be thankful.

Her keys were still in her pocket and thankfully she'd left her purse locked safely in her car. "We have to contact the police. But I think I lost my phone in the lake."

"Your phone's in my bag on the boat. Sorry, I forgot to mention it. You'd dropped it so I picked it up. But I left all my stuff on the deck when I jumped in after you."

"You didn't bring your car on the ferry?"

"I don't have a car and I left my motorcycle back in Toronto because I heard you were expecting storms up here all weekend."

Motorcycle? It was all she could do not to imagine his dark eyes peering through a helmet visor.

"Then how were you planning on getting around the island?"

"Taxis. Transit." He shrugged. "It was a very spontaneous trip. But I'm good at finding my way around, and I don't tend to plan things too tightly. Spontaneous works pretty well for me."

Well, that made one of them. Typical city dweller. With a permanent population of just a few thousand, Manitoulin Island was actually one of the few places left where hitchhiking was still many people's transit of choice. But good luck thumbing a ride if you were a stranger from Toronto. A very tall, very attractive stranger at that.

Stop right there, Meg. Before you get all swoony over him, keep in mind that he's also the kind of reckless man who rides a motorcycle and leaps off moving ferries. Not to mention his life's work is writing about criminals. He's absolutely perfect for that one moment when your life's in mind-numbing danger. But not the kind of man you'd count on to be there the morning after. Let alone the kind that a sensible woman could consider building a life with.

No, a man like that might get her pulse racing. But she already had one man in her life whose risk-taking and adventurous spirit left her pacing the floors at night wondering if he was going to come home safely—her brother, Benji. The last thing she needed was another one.

"So, I'm guessing you're heading back to the mainland tomorrow? The island is hardly a hot-bed of criminal activity."

He shrugged. "My boss doesn't expect me back until Monday. So I'll probably try to find a hotel room somewhere, then chase a few hunches before I head back home. Maybe spend some time boating or fishing too."

Well, if he'd come all this way to find a connection between the island and a serial killer, he could expect to go home empty-handed. The island rumor mill was so well oiled it was impossible to so much as ding a mailbox without the whole island knowing. It was hard to believe someone could be hiding a big, dark secret on Manitoulin Island. And she still wasn't about to let him interview her for the newspaper, not even about her ferry attack, even if he had just saved her life. If what had happened to her family after her brother's accident had taught her anything, it was that small-town gossip could be insidious, unfair and so packed full of lies that even the most innocent person didn't have a shovel big enough to dig his way out from under it.

She didn't even want to guess what would happen if prospective brides searched her name online and discovered she was linked with something as gruesome as an investigation into a potential serial killer. Obviously she'd cooperate with the police and do whatever she could to help make sure her attacker was brought to justice. But she could also count on the police—especially the island cops—not to release her name to the public. She could hardly say the same for the press.

Her attacker might not have taken her life, but the resulting story could still kill her business.

"Well, good luck finding a hotel room on such short notice. My brother has a pretty decent sport's shop, though, if you want to rent a boat. It's on the other side of the island. Something tells me the two of you are cut from the same cloth." The kind that came with far too many warning labels.

He grinned, then ran a hand ran through his tousled wet hair.

Oh Lord, why are the good-looking ones always the most dangerous?

She started picking her way along the shore-line. "Now, come on. Civilization, such as it is, is this way."

He picked up the life ring and slung it over one shoulder. "Would you like my boots?"

"No, thanks. They're way too big for me and there's no point us both getting sore feet. Besides, my little brother and I grew up here. We practically spent our childhood running around barefoot." At least he hadn't offered to carry her. She wasn't sure she could handle the embarrassment, or the rush it would bring to her already exhausted chest.

"The good news is that we're not that far from town," she went on. "We'll pick up my car at the ferry and then drive to the police station in the middle of the island. It's about half an hour away. I'll need to check in with the wedding party too. But under the circumstances, a quick phone call to the bride will just have to do, until we've talked to the police. I wish we'd been able to let the police know before everyone disembarked." The serial killer had probably just walked off the boat into the general population.

Jack frowned. "Why would we have to drive halfway across the island to get to a police station?"

"The closest town doesn't have a police station. You're in Northern Ontario now. Most towns up here are barely more than a few stores and handful of streets." She slid over a fallen tree. "But there's a very popular diner just on the edge of town. There's a good chance we'll find a cop in there. We'll try that first. Even if there isn't a cop there, we can at least call the station and ask if they want us to come in or if they'll send someone to us."

Although the last thing she was going do was incite island-wide panic by walking into the diner and announcing a possible serial killer had just arrived on the ferry. The gossip mill would be abuzz before she'd even manage to get creamer in her coffee. No, there was a way to handle things in a place like this. Go to the police. Have a quiet word. Trust them to handle it. Jack had said the Raincoat Killer liked his victims isolated. Well, this whole island was full of isolated places. But it was also full of people who understood hunters.

"What can you tell me about the victims?" she asked. "Were any of them connected to the island?"

"Not that I know of. Kristy Hooper was studying musical theater and the performing arts. The killer appeared to have broken into her dorm room through the fire escape, possibly looking to rob her. The police think she came home and interrupted him, so he hit her over the head with a lamp. Two different witnesses saw someone in a raincoat on the fire escape that night.

"About a month later, a florist, Eliza Penn, was run over in a back alley leaving work. The car was stolen. Security footage showed the killer wore gloves and a raincoat.

"Then just two weeks ago, another student, Shelly Day, was stabbed. Her landlord found her. I went on a walk-through of the crime scene. It was pretty violent. This one had the clearest security footage too. The killer actually walked right into the lobby of her apartment building, in a raincoat, waited until someone was leaving and grabbed the door to let himself in. Of course, there's no footage of the actual murder, but the timing matches up with the time of death, and everyone else shown entering the building has been accounted for. Someone let a potential serial killer into their building and didn't even notice.

"That's when I stormed into the police station and urged my contacts it was time to go public, and warn people this killer was out there. They said the evidence was circumstantial and they didn't want to create a panic. So I went to my editor, Vince, and talked him into running the story. I thought I was saving lives."

His words were flat, matter-of-fact, like a newsman reading off a press release. Was there something more to this than he was telling her? She caught a depth of emotion in the recesses of his eyes. Sadness. Frustration. Along with the unspoken question *How are you connected to all this?*

She wished she knew.

The trees gave way to an unpaved road. A dilapidated convenience store came into view. Its windows were covered in posters for unsavory movies and advertisements for pornography, live bait and lottery tickets. Two teenaged boys sat on the front step, a mass of badly done body piercings and haphazard tattoos, passing a bottle in a brown paper bag back and forth. Kenny and Stuart Smythe. Kenny was eighteen and had been expelled from the island's only high school for fighting and selling drugs. His brother, Stuart, was three years younger and rapidly heading in the same direction. A lot of people were looking forward to the day the young men hopped a bus off the island to find trouble in a big city, somewhere else and far away.

She wasn't. As long as they were here, in the fishbowl of a small community, there was a chance someone would get through to them. At least, that's what she prayed.

Meg smiled politely at the boys and kept walking.

Jack touched her elbow. "Shouldn't we use their phone?"

She shook her head. "Trust me, we're better off heading to the diner."

"Hey, Meg!" Kenny hollered behind her. "You look like dirt! You and your boyfriend fall off a boat?"

Right, Jack was still carrying the life ring. Stuart snickered. Meg kept walking.

"Hey, dude!" Kenny's voice was slurred, either from alcohol or his infected lip piercing. "Who are you? Why are you covered with mud?" More laughter. When stupid kids were that drunk and high, they thought everything was funny. "You sure you want to be seen in public with a girl that messed up? You do know her little brother killed a guy?"

White-hot anger shot like an arrow up Meg's spine. No, she was not going to give them the satisfaction of a response. They were just stupid, drunk, drugged-up teenagers who didn't know what they were talking about and were just trying to get a reaction. Her fingers clenched into fists. Angry tears filled her eyes. No wonder she still felt trapped by the past. Kenny and Stuart had practically been babies when Benji nearly died in that accident, fourteen years ago, and yet here they were, catcalling her about the terrifying moment that had filled her nightmares ever since.

She kept walking. Jack didn't.

"Come on. Trust me, it's not worth it."

Jack's boots planted themselves firmly. "Gentlemen, I think you should apologize to Ms. Duff."

Stuart glanced uncertainly at his older brother. Kenny laughed. "Oh yeah? And what if we don't?"

Jack's stare grew harder. A grin that was anything but cheerful crossed his lips. Here was a man who'd probably seen more than his fair share of rude, drunk teenagers and wasn't the slightest bit bothered by seeing two more—or, apparently, by the prospect of putting them in their place. For a second it seemed as if Kenny was actually going to try and stare him down. But Stuart scrambled backward up the steps and pulled his brother by the hood until he followed him.

"Whatever." Kenny shrugged. "Sorry if you

can't take a joke. But just so you know, Meg, your brother just got arrested for stealing McCarthy's dog."

The door clanged shut behind them.

"Poor idiots." She rolled her eyes. "Don't listen to them, please. I just hope they get the help they need before they end up in serious trouble." She kept walking. Jack matched her pace. "Thank you for standing up for me. I just didn't have it in me for another fight. Their father owns the store and he's just as bad, which is why I wasn't about to use his phone. I guarantee that if you called the police on them for underage drinking, by the time the cops got here the boys would be gone and their dad would swear he hadn't seen them all day."

The dirt road turned to pavement beneath their feet. Small stores and businesses lined the street ahead of them. She couldn't see the docks, but judging by how busy the street was up ahead, the ferry must have arrived on schedule. They passed a couple of people, strangers. She smiled, nodded, but didn't make eye contact. Two muddy people walking down the street, one of them carrying a life ring, were sure to set tongues wagging. The smartest move right now was to get to the police and file a report. The diner was only steps away, just across the street. It was a main hangout for cops, but even if there were none there, she was sure the owner would let her use the phone discreetly. Not to mention probably pouring her some coffee.

"Meg. About your brother. Does he actually have a criminal record?"

She stopped so suddenly he nearly fell on top of her. Her eyes darted down the street in both directions. Was anyone close enough to overhear him? Not that she could tell. "You're not seriously going to listen to those two, are you?"

He sighed, and for a moment she could almost see an imaginary microphone appearing in his hand. "Look, I promise I won't include it in my article unless it's relevant to the story. But I wouldn't be doing my job if I didn't at least research the possibility your brother could be connected to what just happened to you."

No. This couldn't wait. It had to be said, and it had to be said now.

"Come here." She stepped backward into an empty lot, and behind a Dumpster. "We'd better get this out before we go into the diner. Because I'm not about to say this twice." Her hands snapped to her hips. His eyebrow arched, but she didn't dare let herself back down.

"Now, you listen here, Jack Brooks, crime reporter from Toronto. I'm still not entirely sure why you're up here on the island, or what you're trying to accomplish. But I do know one thing for certain—I have more than enough to deal with in my life right now. So if you start going around stirring up trouble for me and my brother, please believe me when I say I won't have anything to do with you."

FOUR

Fire flashed in her eyes. Jack felt his chest tighten, as the depth of her emotion tugged at something deep inside him. Compassion? Concern? For the first time in his career, the journalist found himself struggling to find the right words to fit his thoughts. All he knew was he could feel the urge to wrap his arms around her surging through his veins, making him want things he could never have. Like the feel of her head tucked safely into the curve of his throat as he promised her he'd never do anything that would ever hurt her.

Don't let yourself get emotionally compromised, Jack. You still have a job to do and your future depends on your ability to stay objective. Even if you did just save this woman's life.

His career was hanging by a thread; he'd just witnessed an attack he believed to be by the very serial killer whom he'd risked everything to expose. Plus, he'd promised the Lord, years ago, he'd never again let his feelings compromise the truth of a story. No matter how strong those feelings might be.

"My little brother is one of the kindest, most generous, most bighearted men you'll ever meet." She was practically hissing. "Benji loves God and other people more than anyone I know. He'd practically treat our home like a free hotel to every sports nut coming through the island if I let him."

Oh, if he had a nickel for every woman he'd heard arguing that her brother, son or husband was really a good guy, while the man was being dragged off by the police for committing some violent crime for the umpteenth time.

He took a step back and crossed his arms. "I'll ask you again, does your brother have a criminal record?"

"No!" Her voice rose. "Years and years ago, when Benji was only fifteen, he and a friend named Chris Quay were in a terrible snowmobile accident. Chris died. Benji just barely managed to pull through. Yeah, the police questioned him, because that's what happens when a kid dies. The fact that they followed procedure doesn't make it anything other than what it was—a horrible, tragic accident. But in the minds of some people, that was enough to taint his reputation for the rest of his life."

"I don't understand."

"Of course you don't! You're from the big city,

where nobody knows their neighbors' business, let alone cares if the person filling up their gas tank ever got questioned by police for reckless driving." She ran both hands through her hair and let it fall back around her heart-shaped face. "But it's a whole other world on the island. Do you know how many people live in most of these towns? Hundreds. That's all. And most of the families have been here for several generations. Reputations run deep, because families tend to know each other through work, or school, or because their grandparents built some important building." She pressed her hand against her chest and took in a deep breath.

"So, you're saying your brother wasn't arrested for stealing a dog?"

Both her hands shot up in the air, as if she were fighting the urge to punch an imaginary enemy. "No! My brother's a bit scatterbrained sometimes. But he's never been arrested for anything. Including stealing."

"But the young man just said—"

"I don't know what Benji did today. I haven't seen him since breakfast. But I guarantee he did not steal anyone's dog. Especially not Bert McCarthy's! The man's in his eighties and probably made it through his whole life without once giving anyone the benefit of the doubt. Three years ago, we had this really heavy, unexpected snowfall in October. Benji was coming home from the shop and didn't have his snow tires on. He got halfway down the hill by McCarthy's, hit black ice, and spun out. Took out a huge chunk of the fence. Benji apologized several times. He felt absolutely terrible. He paid for all the repairs and then some. But still, McCarthy wanted the police to charge him. The police wouldn't. So McCarthy took it through civil court. When the civil court determined Benji had more than paid what he owed, McCarthy took it up through the court of public opinion."

Jack frowned. If she was being honest, then this would be on public record. All it would take was a quick background check. "Well, I'm sure your brother will tell me his side of the story when I interview him."

She barked out a laugh. "No. I'm sorry, Jack. But you will never interview Benji. I already told you, I don't want you writing about us. Not because I'm not grateful for the way you helped me, but because I'm not about to open myself up to gossip any further than I already have. I just want to put this whole thing behind me. Not have every nervous bride who searches my name online, for the rest of my life, wondering if she really wants someone linked to a murderer as her wedding planner.

"If you want to incite mass panic by announcing

there's now a serial killer on the island, I can't stop you. But you're just a reporter, not the police, and as far as I'm concerned, what I need right now is a cop." She started past him, then stopped again. "And while you're at it, please leave the life ring here. I appreciate that you didn't want to leave it in the woods. But it's bad enough that we're walking through town wet and muddy, without having to look like the survivors of a shipwreck."

Jack watched her walk away, across the street toward the striped awning of the diner. Frustration boiled in his veins. Who was she to doubt his professional ethics? Or to tell him what he could and could not write? He sighed. This whole mess was so much more complicated than she realized. The fact of the matter was he didn't need her permission to write about what had happened on the ferry. He'd been there. He'd seen it. He'd come face-to-face with her would-be killer.

And he'd already risked his career to see this killer exposed.

No, her reluctance to see her name in print wasn't actually going to stop him from writing this article. It didn't matter, couldn't matter, how beautiful her face was, or what kind of heartstrings it tugged in him when she looked up into his eyes. He had a responsibility to report the truth, and that's what he was going to do. Besides, it wasn't as if he needed quotes from her. Once they both filed their police reports, all he had to do was report whatever the police said, and then he had a story.

Dear Lord, please help her to understand it isn't personal. I'm just a man with a job to do.

He checked the life ring for damage and found a crack as long as his palm. The ferry wouldn't want it back. He tossed it into the Dumpster. Then he followed her across the street.

She was standing in front of the diner window. When he noticed that her shoulders were shaking, his heart dropped. Was she crying? Had he really upset her that deeply? He stepped closer, his heart lifting unexpectedly as the bubbly sound of laughter filled his ears. Her eyes were alight with joy at a joke whose source he couldn't begin to guess.

"Are you okay?" he asked.

She nodded. "You know how Kenny said my brother was arrested for stealing a dog?" She tapped her fingers on the glass. "Look."

Two men were sitting in a booth by the window. One was a middle-aged, uniformed cop with a bushy red mustache. The other was built like a lumberjack with a short brown beard and blue eyes that twinkled as he glanced up and saw Meg. Her brother? Probably. A Siberian-husky puppy sat on the seat beside him. The men took turns feeding it bits of donut.

"Come on. Come meet my brother." She ran through the doorway, sending the bells chiming and crashing as she went, and Jack had to grab the door with his fingertips to keep it from closing on him.

Benji pushed the dog onto the floor, where it slid under the table. Meg dropped into the booth beside her brother.

"Sis!" Her brother's voice boomed through the room. "You look half-drowned. What happened? Why didn't I see you get off the ferry? And where on earth are your shoes?"

Meg glanced around the crowded diner. The light dimmed from her eyes, replaced by a look so serious the smiles instantly faded from the men's faces. "How about you settle up the tab, and then I'll fill you in somewhere quieter than this?" She turned to the cop and lowered her voice even further. "I have to file a police report. I'm afraid something happened on the ferry."

The cop sat back. Benji nodded slowly, then raised his hand and waved at a gray-haired waitress, who in turn nodded and headed for the cash register. Benji wrapped one large arm around his tiny sister's shoulders. A totally unconvincing smile slid across her face.

"Sorry, I should be doing introductions. Jack Brooks, I'd like you to meet Officer Stephen Burne and my brother, Benjamin Duff, the dastardly dog thief. Watch out, Benji—Jack's a reporter from *Torchlight News* in Toronto."

Was she actually making fun of him? No, she was probably just frightened and trying to break the tension. The least he could not was not make things harder for her.

"Nice to meet you." Jack shook hands around the table.

Benji smiled widely. He pumped Jack's hand. "I didn't steal Harry. He just showed up at the sports store this morning and wanted to hang out. I hopped in the truck to come meet the ferry and see if you wanted to grab some food, Meg, and Harry jumped in for the ride. After I parked the car, Officer Burne came over and told me Bert McCarthy called the police accusing me of dognapping."

Burne rolled his eyes. "Your brother's agreed to return the dog to McCarthy tonight. Old coot is lucky we don't charge him for letting his dog run around town without a collar on."

The waitress raised a bill in their direction. The officer opened his wallet, but Benji waved him off. "No, this one's on me. Harry ate most of the donuts anyway."

The reporter watched as Benji went over to the counter and settled the bill. Normally Jack could get a lot out of watching someone do the simplest things, which was what made meeting Benji so perplexing. There was just something so easygoing, cheerful and transparent about the large, bearded man. Most people, including Officer Burne, tended to flinch a little when he said he was a reporter. But Benji had just grabbed his hand like a man who had nothing to hide.

Jack's every instinct had flared when that drunken kid blurted out that Meg's little brother might have a history with the law. But now? No, he couldn't believe it was true. While he'd still do a criminal background check on Benji, just to be thorough, somehow he already knew it would come up empty.

"You remember my son, Malcolm?" Burne said. "He and my daughter-in-law, Alyssa, came in on the ferry. He's a rookie cop in Toronto, but he's thinking of moving up here to join his old man. Alyssa's hoping to start her own wedding business. Might give you some competition."

Benji returned to the table with a pair of bright pink flip-flops for Meg, which Jack could only assume he'd managed to borrow from someone while sorting the bill. The four of them headed out of the diner for the relative privacy of Burne's police car. They'd barely gone five steps along the sidewalk before Meg bumped into a young couple, whom she introduced as the bride and groom she'd been escorting on the ferry.

Jack's inner reporter sized them up. The young bride, Rachel, was stunning but in a rather generic way—blond, with a slender, athletic frame and a plastic beauty-pageant smile, which she'd plastered onto her face in an apparent attempt to hide the obvious irritation in her eyes. The groom, Wesley, was skinny and twitchy, with a mop of chestnut curls and small horn-rimmed glasses. Nervous because Meg introduced Jack as a reporter? Because Burne was a cop in uniform? Or simply because he was getting married in two days? It was impossible to tell. But Jack couldn't help noticing how Rachel's fingers clutched her fiancé's arm, and that while everyone smiled politely, a thin tremor of tension ran through the small talk they exchanged. The bride was preoccupied with the reception details and seemed oblivious of Meg's state. No wonder Meg had wanted to get away from them on the ferry. Just five seconds in the company of these two and already he was eager to go.

He also noticed that when the bride asked why Meg hadn't met them at the docks, Meg didn't say a word about being attacked, let alone thrown overboard. She'd only smiled professionally, apologized and promised yet again to call them later.

For some reason that bothered him. Could he really expect her to just spill the story out to this young couple, sharing her troubles and fears two days before what was supposed to be the happiest day of their lives? Even if she was willing to burden them like that, would it really be professionally appropriate? No. Not quite. Yet his whole career was based on knowing that keeping the wrong things to yourself only put other people at risk. At risk of what, though? Did he really think the Raincoat Killer was about to infiltrate their wedding? The bride was young and rather beautiful, after all.

He didn't know. That was the problem. It wasn't as if he'd expected the killer to attack Meg on the ferry either. How could anyone possibly defend herself against an unknown, unseen threat?

Ten minutes later, they were sitting in Burne's police cruiser with the windows up. Not quite the private room Jack would have hoped for, but with the closest police station half an island away, it would have to do. Meg and the officer sat in the front seat. Jack, Benji and Harry the dog were crowded in the back. Burne had called his supervisor into the conversation and was taking copious, conscientious notes as first Meg and then Jack relayed what had happened on the ferry.

"We're going to be calling an emergency meeting in with the various island police services." Burne turned to Jack. "The island actually has more than one police service, including both Aboriginal and provincial forces. It's important that everyone get up to speed. We'll have you two tell your stories and then strategize a response. If there is a serial killer on our island, we'll take every precaution to make sure that people are aware, alert and safe." Then the cop turned back to Meg. "In the meantime, why don't we head back to the ferry and get your car and belongings?"

Jack glanced up through the window toward the overcast sky. Thunder rumbled in the dark and distant clouds. *Thank You, Lord!* After everything he'd gone through in Toronto, the police here looked as though they were taking the threat seriously.

Meg walked slowly through the bowels of the ferry's parking deck. The slap of borrowed flip-flops echoed loudly in an empty room, as dark and silent as catacombs. Something about the claustrophobic space always gave her the creeps. The sight of it now, totally bare except for her car sitting alone in the back row, didn't help matters. Officer Burne walked silently beside her. Everything about the cop radiated how seriously he was taking matters—which somehow didn't help the tight knots of nerves in her chest. What she needed right now was someone to help lighten the mood, not to remind her with every concerned glance of just how terrified she'd been above-deck, not that much more than a couple of hours earlier. But her brother would have been the one most likely to cheer her up, and she'd insisted that Benji return Harry the dog to McCarthy's farm before the cranky old man had a heart attack. Meanwhile, Jack had gone above-deck with a member of the ferry's crew to get his bag.

The backseat of her small blue hatchback was down, and crammed with bags from her shopping trip to the mainland. Burne opened the door for her. "Drive down the ramp and wait for me in the parking lot. I will go check with Mr. Brooks, and then we'll head over to the police station in tandem. Okay?"

"Absolutely. No problem."

He closed the door for her, then patted the roof of her car, as if giving it his stamp of approval. She hid a smile. As jittery as she was, she was sure she could handle driving down a ramp and parking her car just fine. She locked the doors anyway.

Meg started the engine and began inching the car slowly through the ferry. She glanced up to the rearview mirror. Burne was watching. She refused to believe that what had happened on the ferry had been anything other than a random attack. Brutal, terrifying, life-shaking—and yet not the slightest bit personal. Now she would have to focus on healing her frightened heart and trusting it to God so that the killer didn't steal away the peace in her soul. And it would be in the hands of the authorities to protect all of the women on the island by making sure he never struck again. *Dear Lord, help them. Help me.*

She reached the end of the deck and gently pressed the brakes as she eased her car down the ramp. Something rustled behind her seat. Shopping bags fell over, spilling their contents around the car. A dark shadow rose to fill the rearview mirror.

She looked up, and into the deep, menacing hood of an orange raincoat.

FIVE

Jack was halfway down to the car deck when he heard Meg scream. He leapt down the stairs and burst through the door, just in time to see Meg's car lurch forward. The hatchback shot down the ramp and clipped the railing. *Dear Lord, protect her from...* From whatever was making her screams shake the air and tear holes through his heart.

The car hit the bottom of the ramp, spun sideways on the wet pier and plowed into the deck's guardrail. Jack ran toward it. The unmistakable silhouette of a hooded raincoat filled the window. His fear spurred him faster, even as he heard Officer Burne pounding through the ferry behind him. The car door fell open and Meg tumbled out onto the ground.

Her eyes met his, wild with panic. "He's in the car!"

The hooded form disappeared from the back window. Was he crouching? Hiding? Searching for something? Had he hoped she'd drive somewhere secluded where he could secretly and cruelly end her life?

Meg was running toward Jack now. But his eyes were focused on the car.

"Jack!" Meg grabbed his arm.

He pulled away and brushed past her.

"Jack! Stop! What are you doing?"

But he'd already reached the car. No movement from the mess of fallen bags in the back. He lunged into the open driver door. "Get out! Now!"

Nothing. Jack yanked the trunk release lever. The hatchback popped open, spilling packages over the ground.

"Get away from the car, Mr. Brooks!" Officer Burne had arrived behind him now, and Jack was just about to turn when something inside the car caught his eye, sending his pulse pounding in frustration.

"Please," the cop said, "step back and let me do my job!" There was the click of a gun's safety pulling back. "Please, do not make me arrest you."

"There's no one here! There never was." Jack yanked something out from between the seats. Then he turned around, holding it and both hands above his head. It was an empty orange raincoat.

Forty minutes later Jack was sitting at a round table in a small room crowded with a handful of representatives of the various police services. Meg sat across the table. Her eyes bored holes in the surface in front of her. The damage to her car had been nothing more than surface dents. Jack had offered to drive it to the station for her, while Meg went on ahead with Burne.

She hadn't looked his way once since he arrived. Was she upset with him for running past her to the car like that? Surely she realized the danger had been minimal and the potential break in the case had been huge. It wasn't as if he'd put her life in danger. Especially as it turned out there hadn't actually been anyone in the back of her car.

"The raincoat was looped through a worn piece of molding on the sunroof, with a paper clip and a piece of clear fishing line," Jack said. "All things the killer could have found in the back of the car. He then ran the wire under the seat and attached it to the brake so that whenever Ms. Duff hit the brake hard enough the coat would pop up." Terribly simple, but probably terrifying to witness. "It's a cruel trick, which marks a distinct change of behavior from what we already know about the so-called Raincoat Killer."

Heads nodded around the table. These cops weren't just listening; they were taking him seriously. Big change from how his journalistic research had been treated by law enforcement in Toronto. *A very nice change.* Then again, the cops in Toronto had been investigating the deaths of three seemingly unconnected women in a city of millions. Considering everything even he'd seen and heard in his years as a reporter, it was no surprise the Toronto police got a bit jaded sometimes.

Thankfully, life in a small town was a whole world away from that.

"Mr. Brooks, do you know why a serial killer from Toronto would possibly come all the way up here?" Burne asked.

The island police had apparently contacted investigators in Toronto, who'd promised to send up their records tomorrow. Until then, Jack found himself in the unlikely position of being the closest thing police services had to an expert on the deadly killer now stalking their remote, idyllic island.

"No, sir." Jack leaned his forearms on the table. "I don't know for certain. I can tell you there were Manitoulin Island ferry schedules in all three of the crime scenes. One had today's afternoon ferry circled." He glanced toward Meg, willing her to meet his eyes. She didn't. "That same crime scene also had a flyer for Ms. Duff's business."

Big blue eyes looked up and met his, winsome and fringed with dark lashes. His arms ached to give her the hug he'd neglected to give her after she crashed her car. She'd reached out for him. She'd wanted his support. But then there'd been the police, and questions to be answered, and he'd wanted to figure out exactly what the killer had done to her car....

"So you decided to hop on that specific ferry and come all the way up here, just in case there was a connection?" The question came from a female officer in the corner, whose name he hadn't quite caught. He couldn't tell whether she was impressed or amused. "Your editor must have a lot of faith in you."

There was an unsettled feeling in his stomach. "Actually, Officer, my boss gave me a few days off and told me to let him know how the hunch panned out." The cop was still staring at him. "I've already had it pointed out to me that I could have just phoned around, instead of making the trip. But it's one thing to see a picture of an island on a flyer or to hear a stranger's voice on the phone. It's a whole different thing to walk around a place, see it for yourself and get a feel for it."

Meg rubbed her eyes. Officer Burne said something to her that Jack couldn't quite hear.

Then the officer held up his hand. "Sorry to interject, but Ms. Duff's had quite the ordeal today, and it seems like everyone's done questioning her for now. So if no one has any objections, maybe we can thank her for her time and let her go home?"

There was a general nod and murmur around the table. Then Burne walked Meg out.

"Excuse me." Jack glanced around the table. "I need a moment." There was an interminable pause, some hushed conferring and then somebody called a fifteen-minute break. Jack forced himself not to run after her.

He found Meg standing outside. Her face was lit in the faint glow of the sun setting behind dark orange clouds. Her arms were wrapped around herself. Her eyes were turned toward the dying light and filled with a look so haunted that Jack's every impulse was to sweep her up into his arms.

He shoved his hands into his pockets. "You leaving?"

She nodded. "Officer Burne is just checking on something and then he's going to follow me home." She let out a long breath. "I'm still in the clothes I was wearing when I fell overboard. While they were dry enough to give a statement in, they hardly feel clean. And anyway, I need to check in with Rachel, and she's hardly an easy bride to deal with." Her shoulders fell. "Plus, I'm starving. I haven't had anything to eat since lunch, which now feels like a day ago."

Jack glanced at his watch. It was after seven. He still needed to call his editor, Vince, fill him in on what had happened and tell him that he was about to deliver one hefty knockout of a story, which had the potential to change everything.

Even though the beautiful, extraordinary woman

standing next to him now was probably going to hate him for it.

His chest ached. Everything he knew about her, everything he'd seen since meeting her, told him that Meg was a strong, confident woman who was more than capable of rising above any fallout or negative attention, which might possibly come from being named as the sole survivor of a serial killer. Sure, his story might raise a few uncomfortable questions from her prospective clients or send some press headed her way for a while. But it wasn't as if it would ruin her. Why couldn't she see that the story of what had happened today needed to be made public?

Besides, it wasn't as if he had much of a choice.

"Meg?" She turned toward him, standing so close the tips of her flip-flops nearly brushed against his toes. "What would you say if, when I was done here, we met up for dinner somewhere? To talk through everything that's happened."

Her forehead wrinkled. "As two people? Or as a reporter and the person he's trying to interview?"

"Can't it be both?"

Meg's eyes searched his face for a long moment. She shook her head. "No."

"No to dinner or no to the interview?"

"No to both." Her voice was firm. "Like I told you before, I will be extremely thankful every day of my life that you were there and jumped overboard to save me. But I will not help you wreck my life by writing about it."

He could feel the tension rising in the back of his neck. She had to know how the press worked. She couldn't be that naive. "You do realize that I have to tell my editor what happened here today, and he will expect me to write about it. I don't need your permission. I saw a madman in an orange raincoat throw you off that ferry with my very own eyes."

Her arms crossed. "Trust me, I know all about what reporters can and can't do. Like too many people, I guess, I learned the hard way. But it means I know that any editor worth his ink is going to want to make sure that someone is willing to back up your story. I've already asked the police not to leak my name to the press, which leaves me as your only corroborating source. If I make it clear that I will not confirm the facts of your story, would your editor still run it?"

Seriously? His jaw dropped. Did she have any idea just how much that would further undermine his already shaky position with the paper?

The door opened and Officer Burne came outside. He nodded to Jack.

Meg managed a smile. "Goodbye, Jack. If I don't see you again before you leave the island, I'll email your paper about whether or not I have any record of those three women ever contacting me. Thanks again for everything." She turned and headed for her car so quickly he couldn't shake the feeling she was actually running away from him.

"Don't mention it. See you around." He shoved his hands into his pockets and tried not to watch her go.

SIX

Meg gripped the steering wheel with both hands. Her eyes darted back up to the mirror. The police officer was still there, as he had been for the last twenty minutes, following her just two car lengths back. *Keep breathing, Meg. Just keep breathing.*

Her car crested a hill on the narrow road, and the familiar cluster of streamers came into view. The old, dented tree was virtually covered in multicolored ribbons, faded from years of being battered and tossed by the weather. The large, unmistakable memorial telegraphed to everyone who passed—*something bad happened here, someone died and we're never going to forget.*

Tears threatened to spill from her eyes. She blinked hard. Then she spoke aloud in the empty car. "It is well, it is well with my soul."

Fourteen years since the accident and yet with every winter school-safety assembly, or fresh pot of coffee at the first snowfall of the season, the story of how her big, strong brother nearly died remained alive in the community's mind.

Some years back, someone would say, *two reckless teenaged boys went snowmobiling down this very hill. They weren't sticking to the paths like they were supposed to. Guess they were in a hurry to get somewhere. Then a transport truck came along and hit them both so hard they never saw it coming. One boy spent months in a coma. The other boy...* The speaker's head would shake. *He wasn't so lucky.*

Chris Quay had been eighteen—three years older than her brother, Benji—and in so many ways the apparent opposite of his slender, nervous cousin, Wesley, who was getting married this weekend. The only similarity she saw was that Chris had the same curly chestnut hair and green eyes as Wesley, though in Chris they had been paired with a reckless, adventurous, daredevil spirit Meg had been foolish enough to find attractive. She could still remember the smirk on his face as he and her brother had sped off together. Still remembered watching the color drain from her mother's face as she'd taken the phone call from the police. Media reports, of which there were many, said Chris had died on impact. Some reporters wanted the truck driver charged. Others wanted Benji charged. In the end, no one was charged.

Her brother spent almost two years in and out of hospital, learning how to make his arms and legs work again. Not that it showed now. If anything, having a brush with death had made him even bolder, braver, sending him flying down black-diamond ski hills and jumping out of airplanes with parachutes on his back—seemingly oblivious of how every adventurous leap made his sister pace the floor in worry, begging God to keep her brother safe.

Benji even seemed to enjoy being a community-wide object lesson. He spoke to students about the importance of sports safety. His sports-equipment store was flourishing. Many people would think of going nowhere else for helmets, harnesses and life jackets. While islanders didn't forget, they were willing to forgive—most of them anyway.

And Meg had learned never to let herself fall in love with a thrill seeker. She already loved one man—her precious brother—who seemed determined to keep throwing himself full throttle into every adrenaline rush he could find, while she did the worrying and panicking for the both of them.

And now the flurry of butterflies beating against her insides whenever Jack was around proved she still hadn't learned her lesson. Watching him charge past her toward the hooded shape in her car had made that even clearer. Here was a man who didn't even have the protection of a badge or a gun and yet spent his life relentlessly pursuing the most dangerous of criminals with nothing more than a microphone.

Yes, she admired him for that. Yes, she respected him. But that didn't mean she could take the risk of letting herself fall for him.

The bungalow was long and low, with aluminum siding, a sweeping front porch and a neglected For Sale sign that had sat on the front lawn since their parents retired to Florida five years ago. The house had been left to the children, and Benji had said once it sold he would use his share of the proceeds to sail solo around the world…so, of course, Meg let every Realtor on the island know she had no intention of selling until he settled down.

She'd left the front door unlocked without thinking twice. Most people did on the island. But now Burne insisted on doing a complete walk-though of every room, to make sure no one had broken in while she was gone. Only when he was certain there were no killers under the beds or lurking in the closets did the officer help unload her bags into the large front room she used as an office. Finally he left her alone, saying he'd sit out front in his car until her brother came home. She didn't know whether to be grateful for his concern or nervous that a police officer thought she needed to be babysat.

The house's main floor and basement were almost mirror images of each other, with two bedrooms, a large bathroom and a living room in each. Since their parents moved out, the siblings treated the house as two separate apartments, sharing only the large, sunlit kitchen on the main floor. Tasteful, well-kept order reigned on Meg's floor, where the beautiful beige and blue living room doubled as a meeting space for clients. But every inch of the basement apartment was pure Benji—cluttered, friendly and loud.

She washed the lake water out of her hair and got dressed again in a well-worn pair of jeans, simple T-shirt and soft blue sweatshirt. Then she called Rachel.

Not only was Rachel's wedding the most expensive she'd ever arranged, but it was also the most rushed. Rachel was barely twenty, a dance student in college, and didn't seem much older than the troubled young woman Meg had taught in Sunday school years ago. Her stoic grandmother lived in a retirement home overlooking the stunning glass-and-wood waterfront pavilion her late husband had built. She was what was considered old, respectable money—the closest thing the island had to royalty. And since the island loved nothing more than to gossip about its most important citizens, that meant that everyone knew the story of the family tragedy.

When Rachel's mother had run away from home at eighteen, with the petty mainland drug dealer who was Rachel's father, she was cut off entirely, in the hopes that financial hardship would bring her to her senses. It didn't work. When Rachel was twelve, she was found by the police huddled in the backseat of a car. Her mother died of a drug overdose that night in hospital. Her father was long gone.

Rachel's grandmother had clearly decided not to make the same mistake twice. She'd taken her estranged granddaughter in to live with her and given the reputedly brilliant but high-strung child every advantage that had been denied to her mother. But when Rachel had called from the university to say she and her boyfriend, Wesley, were heading to London, to follow her dreams as a dancer, her grandmother had insisted the young couple get married first, respectfully, in the island community that was home.

"I thought you were going to meet us when the ferry docked." The young bride's voice was breathless over the phone line now, her words seeming to battle each other to get out. "You know I barely know anyone on this island and Wesley hasn't stepped foot here since he was a kid."

Well, if you'd taken the time to actually come up here instead of just barking orders over the phone—

She tried to say sorry, but Rachel's words were speeding up so quickly now she couldn't even find a chance to interject.

"Fortunately the best man was able to find the address for the hotel, and Wesley wanted to see the yacht we rented for the honeymoon, so we decided to all split up and meet back at the hotel later anyway. But that doesn't change the fact that you stood me up and then randomly showed up on the street looking like you'd just gone swimming in mud. What's going on? Are you okay? Should I be worried?"

Meg forced herself to take three deep breaths. No, all she'd promised to do was meet Rachel on the mainland for a wedding-dress fitting. The vintage-style knee-length dress had been custom-made and looked like something out of a musical. The fact that the wedding party had also ferried in from the city that day was just the way things had happened to work out. The island only had one afternoon ferry. "Everything's fine. I just had a problem on the ferry. But it's sorted now and it doesn't need to concern you—"

"I just drove past the pavilion and it's smaller than I realized it was going to be. Are you certain the second floor is going to be okay for the reception? You do know my grandfather dedicated it to my grandmother."

"Yes, and there's more than enough room. The

site is perfect. The restaurant is exquisite, and the view of the water is spectacular. You'll see for yourself at the rehearsal dinner tomorrow, but I can walk you through before then. We're meeting up just after lunch tomorrow. There should be plenty of time."

"You're sure the floral centerpiece is going to work in that room? I want it to be huge."

Oh, it would be. The stone fountain would take three deliverymen to set it up inside the pavilion before the decorators covered it in wildflowers. "Trust me. You're going to have a beautiful wedding."

"I think we should meet tomorrow morning and go over everything one last time," Rachel said, "the decorations, the menu, the rehearsal, everything—just to make sure we're all on the same page."

The day before the wedding? What could she possibly think they could change at that point?

"We need this to be special for Wesley, after all," Rachel added. "He had a really tragic childhood. Did you know his only cousin died up here when he was little?"

Guilt pierced Meg's heart. So Rachel didn't know Meg's brother was the one who had been in that accident too? Yes, the narcissistic young bride had lived on the island a few years as a teenager before heading off to college in Toronto at just seventeen. But maybe someone that self-centered and inwardly focused just didn't register the lives and issues of others. It would certainly explain why she'd never once mentioned the connection to Meg. But then presumably Wesley didn't remember Benji's family name either.

Considering they'd practically invited the entire island to the wedding, someone was bound to mention it. A thought tickled at the back of Meg's mind. Who would want a few hundred strangers coming to their wedding anyway? Let alone someone like Rachel. Was the whole thing an exercise in making her grandmother happy? Giving the old woman a big, fancy event, with all of her friends, so she'd keep signing the checks and funding Rachel's dreams? How sad. No wonder Rachel was a bit manic about the parts of her wedding she could control.

"Sure. Tomorrow morning would be fine." She could hold off running errands for a couple of hours. It would give her a chance to say something to Wesley and Rachel in private about his cousin's accident too, before a few dozen gray-haired strangers ambushed him with questions. "You'll bring Wesley?"

She heard the front door slam, and then the sound of too many feet entering her kitchen. Something barked. Meg groaned silently.

"Sure," Rachel said. "I'll bring the whole wedding party."

Meg set down the phone and headed for the kitchen. Benji was standing at the counter with two open pizza boxes. Harry the dog—who for some reason had still not gone home—was running laps around the kitchen. But it was the sight of the very tall, very good-looking reporter sitting in front of a laptop at her kitchen table that made her heart skip a sudden beat.

Jack had one of her business flyers open on the keyboard, but when he saw her come in, he snapped the laptop closed and stood. His eyes searched her face. What was he looking for? A sign as to how she felt about him being there?

Well, the answer would be…conflicted. And way happier to see him there than she was comfortable with.

"Hi, Jack. Welcome to my home."

"Thank you." He held his palms up toward her, as if half expecting to be shot. "I'm here as a friend, not a reporter."

A smile tugged at the corner of her cheeks. Well, that was one piece of good news at least. Although it still didn't explain what he was doing in her kitchen. "How did you know where I live?"

Jack pointed a finger at Benji.

"We ran into each other at the police station," her brother said. "I went there looking for you, but you'd already gone." He pulled a slice of pizza out of the box and folded it in half. "He needs somewhere to stay, sis. Every half-decent place on the island is booked up already."

"I managed to find a room at a motel on the other side of the island," Jack added. "But when I tried telling your brother that, he practically marshaled me into his truck."

Benji gave his sister a meaningful look and rolled his eyes. Yeah, they knew the place. The owner was an off-islander who'd bought the place two years ago and run it into the ground. Chances were he'd have expected Jack to slip him an extra fifty bucks just to get clean sheets.

"You wouldn't want to stay there anyway," Meg said. "They have bedbugs." She sighed and gripped the back of a kitchen chair with both hands. "But I'm not sure where else to direct you." While Manitoulin's entire population was only a few thousand, it was spread among several tiny towns, some well over an hour's drive away from each other.

"Would you be okay if he bunked downstairs?" Benji asked. "I told him that I rented out my spare room all the time to fellow sports nuts, and that you never minded, as long as I cleared it with you first."

Ah. There it was. Her brother collected new friends like rocks on the beach. To be fair, he tended to have excellent taste in people too, and had introduced her to quite a few tourists who'd ended up becoming wedding clients. But normally they were fellow scruffy thrill seekers. Never anyone who made her heart race at the thought of bumping into them over morning coffee.

"Figured it was the least I could do, considering he saved my sister's life," Benji added. "Plus, this guy is way too cool. Did you know he's into bungee-jumping? He's going to come by the store tomorrow to check out the new harnesses."

She turned back to Jack, and tried not to imagine him diving off a cliff headfirst with a rubber band strapped to his ankles. "Welcome. I'm sure Benji will love having someone else living in his man cave this weekend." Not to mention that there was something about the idea of having him sleeping downstairs that made the house feel more secure. She walked over to the pizza. One was extra pepperoni and one was vegetarian. She chose pepperoni.

"Now, why do we still have a dog?" She picked a piece of pepperoni off her pizza and passed it to Harry. He sat for it. The husky looked to be less than four months old and judging by his features was almost certainly purebred. While it was a pretty popular breed in the North, purebreds didn't come cheap. "I thought you were going to take Harry home."

"I did!" Benji said. "But McCarthy wouldn't open the door. I tried to leave him with a neighbor, but he said the old grump doesn't even want him." He slapped his leg twice. Harry bounded over. Benji scratched the dog behind his ears. "Neighbor says the dog was dumped at McCarthy's by some niece from Sudbury who hadn't realized big dogs and small apartments don't mix. Seems like McCarthy wouldn't stop complaining that Harry had too much energy and barked way too much, so he just left him outside hoping he would run away. Only went to the police because someone called and told him they saw Harry in my truck."

Why didn't that surprise her? McCarthy had lost his wife in a car accident when Meg was little. After Chris and Benji's accident, McCarthy had spearheaded the campaign to get Benji thrown in jail. Grief had a way of making some people hold on to the hurt, until it spilled out onto others. Then when Benji had crashed through his fence three winters ago, the old man's hatred for her brother had grown into a full-on vendetta.

"All right," she said, "but the last thing you want is for him to sue you again. How about I take him over? Last I checked, he was still opening the door to me. Then if he doesn't answer, I'll bring Harry back here for the night." And if he did answer the door, she'd try making the old man a generous offer for the dog. Considering that Harry didn't even have a collar on, chances were the neighbor was right. "I'll take my car, and considering how he feels about you, it's probably best you stay home."

Her brother's arms crossed over her chest. "I don't want you going alone, and I sent Burne home."

"I'll go," Jack said. "Just give me a second to get changed into something I didn't go swimming in."

Meg opened her mouth to object, but there were two men staring her down now. "All right. But just because it's late and his farm is pretty remote. I'm going to have to start going places by myself again eventually."

Benji led Jack downstairs. The door to the lower level closed behind them. She leaned her arms against the counter. Taking Jack with her would be much safer—physically speaking. But why did it feel she was putting her heart in jeopardy?

The headlights of her small blue hatchback cut through the darkness. Thick clouds filled the sky above them, blocking out the stars. The weather report was calling for intermittent thundershowers all weekend, the kind of unpredictable weather that could switch in an instant from blazing sun to a raging rain. There was even the chance of a megastorm for Saturday afternoon. Hopefully the happy couple would get a chance to squeeze in a few pictures on the beach before it hit.

Jack was squeezed into the seat beside her. When she'd left the backseat down for Harry, she hadn't realized Jack would end up bunched between the seat and the dashboard. "You know, you can put the seat back. I'm sure Harry can move."

"Thanks. I'm fine." His eyes darted up to the rearview mirror for the tenth time since they'd left her driveway.

She looked but saw nothing except the blackness of the empty, unlit road. "What are you looking for?"

"Your brother told me he thought someone followed him after he left us at the docks. But thanks to the weather, all he really saw were headlights."

Her throat tightened. "And why didn't he tell me that?"

"He didn't want you to worry. He said you worry too much as it is."

Maybe so. But still. The wreaths and ribbons of the crash memorial rose into view. How many times had she passed this spot in the past dozen years? Hundreds? Thousands? How many more until it no longer made her heart twist in her chest?

"Your brother told me all about the accident too." Jack's voice cut into her thoughts. "I'm guessing the press was all over it for months. Must've been hard."

There was a gentleness to his voice she wasn't expecting.

"Reporters used to stake out our home, the hospital, the high school, all while we were still waiting to find out if Benji was going to make it." She shrugged. "A kid was dead and they were looking for someone to blame. Some blamed the truck driver. A lot more blamed Benji, especially because he and Chris weren't wearing helmets. The worst was when some current-affairs television crew went after my father's business. Dad was a mechanic and serviced a lot of snowmobiles. They harassed all his clients, trying to determine if any had accidents because of faulty maintenance. It was a total muckraking. But rumors were enough to scare some people off using him again, especially nonislanders. His business never really recovered."

"That's terrible. I'm really sorry." Jack's hand hovered in the air above her shoulder for a moment, as if he was debating whether or not to give it a squeeze. But instead he dropped it back down to his side, which left her feeling more disappointed than she'd have expected.

She turned off the main road onto the long, winding driveway to McCarthy's farm. The farmhouse was old, with peeling paint and a detached double garage behind it that had seen better days. The lights were off on the main floor. But one lone light flickered faintly in an upstairs window.

Jack unbuckled his seat belt. "It doesn't look like anyone is home."

"Nah." She undid hers, as well. "He's here— he's just stingy about using electricity."

Harry growled softly. Guess he wasn't all that happy to be home. Jack turned around in his seat and ran his hand over the dog's neck. "It's okay, boy."

A shadow moved past the upstairs window, and then a hooded figure stepped up to the glass.

She gasped.

Jack spun forward. "What is it?"

With one hand she reached down for something to hold onto and steady herself. With the other, she pointed up toward the window. An indistinguishable gray shape moved through the upstairs room. The light went out and the house went dark.

It was only then that she realized she'd actually grabbed Jack's arm, just like she might have grabbed onto Benji's.

"What's wrong?" Jack stroked his thumb gently along hers. She imagined he'd intended it as a reassuring gesture, but it was enough to send sparks shooting through her skin.

She pulled away. "This might sound crazy, but I thought that for a second McCarthy was wearing a hood."

SEVEN

The dog was still growling. The sound was unnerving and seemed to be getting louder by the second. Jack exhaled slowly. What if the person who had trailed Benji's truck to the farm earlier had been the Raincoat Killer? What if he'd mistakenly thought this might be where Benji and Meg lived, and had come back later looking for them? Unlikely? Yes. Impossible? Not by a long shot. What some people might consider a mildly paranoid way of assembling the facts was just a natural line of thought for someone in his profession. But there was no reason to tell her that.

"No," he said carefully, "it doesn't sound crazy. An old man, alone in his bedroom in the evening? He could easily have been wearing a hooded bathrobe, or had a blanket over his head."

Her shoulders straightened and determination filled her eyes again. "Come on." She opened her door. "Let's go."

Jack climbed out of the passenger seat, then held

the door open for Harry. "Come on, boy, let's go." The dog crouched lower. His growl deepened. Meg was already halfway to the porch. Okay, then. Jack left the door open and strode after her.

"Mr. McCarthy!" Meg rapped hard on the faded front door. "It's Meg Duff. I've brought your dog back." No answer.

"Not the friendliest fellow, is he?" Jack reached past her and knocked firmly, using the three hard raps that he found people understood as "I'm a professional, and I mean business." They waited. There was creaking, which sounded like someone trying to tiptoe down a very old flight of stairs, followed by the thud of something falling over. He cupped his hands to the window and peered inside. He couldn't see anything. "Mr. McCarthy!" He raised his voice toward the house. "My name is Jack Brooks. We apologize for coming at such a late hour…." He glanced at his watch. It had barely gone nine. Oh well, who knew what time the curmudgeon went to bed? "We'd be happy to just leave your dog wherever is convenient for you—" if they could get the agitated dog to stop growling and climb out of the car "—and leave you in peace. Unfortunately he doesn't have a collar or leash, so we can't tie him to the railing."

Still no answer. Jack looked at Meg. His voice dropped. "Do you think there's something wrong?"

"Honestly?" She snorted. "Probably not. He's a

miserable man who called the police out of spite, but I find it easy to believe he doesn't really want his dog back." Footsteps shuffled from inside the house, but still the door remained stubbornly unanswered. "I honestly think he gets a kick out of inconveniencing people, like making them wait makes him feel important. When we dropped by to pay for his broken fence, we heard him shuffling around inside for a good fifteen minutes before he finally wandered out to his workshop and acted all surprised to see us there. Still, I can understand some of the sourness. It must be lonely out here, all by himself. You can't help feeling sorry for him."

Can't you? Jack's eyes ran over the soft shadows that traced their way along Meg's shoulders. Did that kind of compassion come naturally to her? Or was it born from weeks of pacing hospital hallways? "What do you want to do?"

"Oh, I'm in no hurry to leave. Not after he called the cops on my brother."

There was the clatter of the back door slamming. Meg rolled her eyes, but the look in them was more pity than frustration. "Come on. Let's head around back and talk to him. He'll probably be puttering around his workshop, pretending to be doing something important. One way or the other, it'll get settled."

Jack followed. The detached garage was a

solid concrete block. The carport door was open slightly, leaving a gap of just a few inches at the bottom. A faint yellow light shone from underneath. Had that been on when they arrived?

A shadow moved out from behind the house and disappeared through a doorway at the back of the garage. The door remained open behind him.

They followed. A heavy key chain hung from the knob. They entered a narrow room separated from the main garage by a dividing wall. A workbench ran down one side. The walls hung heavy with gardening implements and two full sets of tools. Light trickled through a doorway in the back, which Jack guessed led into the main garage.

His eyes ran over the meticulously kept space. *Everyone cares about something. It's just a matter of figuring out what.*

Meg knocked on the doorframe. "Hello?"

If only more people remembered to treat each other with the courtesy she did.

"Mr. McCarthy!" Meg cupped her hands around her mouth. "Are you in here?" She walked into the workshop behind Jack. The back of her hand slipped ever so slightly against his, as though she was fighting the urge to take it. "Something feels wrong," she whispered.

"What does?"

"I don't know. It's just, he's inconvenienced us.

He's made us wait. He dragged us out here. Fine. He's made his point. But now it's getting—"

A burst of barking filled the air. The door slammed shut behind them. The keys turned in the lock. Then the room went black.

Jack pulled on the door, shaking it until the knob rattled. It wouldn't budge. "Looks like we're locked in. We're just going to have to walk through the garage and go out through the car door."

He forced his voice to stay calm, which was hard to do with Harry still barking furiously outside. One hand slid up the wall until he found a light switch. He flicked it up, but the room stayed dark. "And the power's off." *So, what was that glow coming from the other part of the garage?*

There was a flicker of light behind him as Meg turned on her cell phone. "I can't get a signal. But that's pretty typical in this part of the island." Her voice was level, with only the faintest quiver giving her anxiety away. Her hand slid onto Jack's arm. He squeezed it for a long moment, feeling her pulse racing through her wrist.

Okay, Lord. She's terrified. And I could really use some help keeping my head right now.

There was the rattle of the garage door closing. *No!* Jack rushed toward the disappearing light, the room growing darker before his eyes. Then the dim light shining from the main garage disappeared too. His hand felt for the doorway—

His shins smacked hard against something on the floor. He pitched forward, nearly landing on top of it. A fallen stepladder. He heard the garage door hit the floor, with a metallic clank that echoed through the concrete space. Now it sounded as though both exits had been closed and locked.

Something creaked in the darkness above him.

"Stay back. There's something else here." *Or someone.*

He dug in his pocket for his cell phone and came up empty. Must've left it in the car. A thin beam from Meg's phone flickered over his shoulder. Jack stepped back as he saw a pair of battered work boots swing through the air toward them. *Lord, have mercy.* He slid his hand onto Meg's and helped her guide the phone's beam upward, up the battered boots and frail legs.

McCarthy's dead body was hanging from the ceiling.

EIGHT

The old man's body was suspended from a beam, a crude noose around his neck. Jack's heart stopped beating as the air he was breathing froze in his chest. *Hanged.* The reporter stood there for a moment, paralyzed. But then he heard a pain-filled gasp slip from Meg's throat and felt her weight shift as her legs began to give way.

Jack pressed both of his heels firmly into the floor. *No, Jack. You're not going to get overwhelmed by this. She needs you to be strong.*

Meg's phone clattered to the floor. He reached for her, gently pulling her into the comfort of a firm and supportive embrace. She fell into his chest and he held her there. His right hand slid down to the curve of her back, his fingers spread along her waist. The other hand brushed against the soft skin at the nape of her neck and curled through her hair. "It's okay." His voice brushed against her ear. "I've got you." She turned her head toward him. He tasted the salt of her tears. "We're going to get out of here. You and me. Okay?"

"He… McCarthy…" Her voice disappeared into a sob. "Who would do such a thing?"

The barking outside turned into a low, threatening snarl. Meg's fingers crept around Jack's neck, pulling him closer still. Their hug deepened. And then she pushed back gently. He let her go. Her phone was on the floor near McCarthy's truck, its thin beam illuminating the bare concrete room. Meg picked it up and shone the light on the sliding garage door. Jack yanked the handle. Then he threw his weight into it. It wouldn't budge. They were all out of exits.

Jack eyed the truck. "We're going to have to bust our way out of here, and I think our best chance is to drive through the garage door. One good hit with the truck and it should fly open."

If the killer was still out there, they'd at least have a big hunk of steel between them and him. The truck's driver's-side door was unlocked. Judging by the key chain they'd seen dangling outside the workshop door, there was probably no use searching the old man's pockets for keys. Hopefully, though, there'd be a spare key somewhere in the truck.

Jack climbed in first. He yanked open the glove compartment, felt around and then looked under the car mat. Nothing. He glanced in the backseat and came up with another toolbox.

Meg climbed in beside him. "Just yank out the starter and I'll hot-wire it."

"You serious?"

"Is there a wrench?"

Jack flung the toolbox lid open. "There is. You sure you can do this?"

"My father was a mechanic, and my brother loses his keys with amazing regularity. Move over and hold the light."

Within moments the starter lay in pieces in her hand. Jack watched as her fingers danced over the wires. The engine roared. "Ready?" Jack nodded, then braced his hands on the dashboard and breathed a prayer for their safety. Meg put the truck in reverse. She gripped the steering wheel with both hands. "Here we go."

The truck surged backward, hitting the garage door with such force it came off the rails and flew through the air behind them. Night sky filled the rearview mirror. Meg hit the brakes. Jack scanned from the driveway all the way to the tree line for any trace of movement. But all he could see was Meg's car sitting—seemingly untouched—exactly where they'd left it. The dark, damp air around them was silent. Even the barking had stopped. He couldn't see where Harry had gone.

"That was amazing what you just did," he said.

"You impress me to no end. Do you have a signal yet? We should call the police."

Meg didn't answer. Her head didn't even turn. Then he noticed just how tightly her fingers were clenching the steering wheel. She stared straight through the gaping hole that once was McCarthy's garage door as if transfixed by the swaying body, illuminated by the truck's headlights.

The rope had been strung around the old man's neck. The stepladder Jack had tripped over lay at his feet. Again, questions filled the reporter's mind, pushing him to think rationally. His journalistic instincts buzzed. *Examine the scene, Jack. What do you see? Bruising on the victim's body. Heavy bruising on his forehead. Okay, any other evidence? No footprints. No sign of a break-in. Nothing to indicate a struggle. Although how does that fit any of the facts?*

"They didn't just kill him, they strung him up." Her teeth chattered. "Nobody here would do this to him.… I'm not saying he didn't have enemies. But they might grumble about him, or take him to court, or maybe even threaten to take a swing at him. But no one would…no one would…"

Her eyes glazed over. He knew this look. Sometimes when people were terrified they closed up like a steel trap, as if trying to shut themselves away from whatever had just scared them witless.

"Meg, look at me," he said gently but firmly.

"Look at me and not at him." He reached for her hand and gently tried to pull it from the steering wheel. "Come on, we're going to go back to your car, and I'm going to call the police." She was going into shock, and probably couldn't even hear him.

She grabbed her mouth as a muffled scream slipped through her fingers. In an instant, Jack saw why. The dead body turned slowly as it swayed. There was a piece of paper taped to McCarthy's back with something written across the back in large block letters. *MEG.*

NINE

Anger flashed in the recesses of Jack's heart as the desire for justice burned through him like a flame. Who did something like this? What kind of monster would tape her name on the back of a corpse?

Tears coursed from Meg's eyes. Jack leapt out of the truck, ran around to her side of the truck and opened the driver's-side door.

"Come on, hon. Let's get you out of here." He slid his left arm under her knees and the other around her shoulders. Then he lifted her gently off the seat, cradling her in his arms. Her fingers slid slowly from the steering wheel, but her body stayed so stiff he'd have thought she was frozen. There was the same lost look in her eyes that he'd seen in the face of crime victims and witnesses far too many times before. *Help her, Lord. She's shutting down. I can't reach inside and settle her terrified heart, Lord, but You can. Help her. Help me help her.*

He carried her around to the front of the house and sat carefully on the front steps, holding her against him. "It's going to be okay. I promise." He pressed her hand against his chest. "Meg? Can you feel my heartbeat?" Considering how hard it was thudding, he wouldn't be surprised if she could even hear it. "Focus on counting the beats. Okay? Just that. One. Two. One. Two." Her breath came hard and fast on his throat. His fingers stroked her back, from the base of her skull down to the gentle curve of her lower back. "Now you need to calm your breathing. I know it's hard. Just focus on my breath, slow and steady. Breathe along with me."

Slowly, her fists unclenched. Then her hands ran up around his neck, holding him to her like a lifeline; the simple act tugged at his heart, pulling on desires he'd never let himself feel before. He wanted to protect her. Help her. Be strong for her. Keep her safe. He closed his eyes, feeling her breath on his face, and her lips just inches away from his own.

Then he felt her pull back. He let her go and opened his eyes. "You okay?"

She nodded. "Yes. Thank you." Her body slid away from his slightly. "I've had panic attacks, little ones, since Benji's accident. It's a fear thing. But normally I can calm myself down. I don't usually freeze like that."

He brushed the hair back from her face, cupping her cheek for just a moment. "It's okay. It's a completely normal reaction. Trust me, I've seen a lot of people freaking out far more at the sight of far less." She rolled her head around slowly on her shoulders. He pulled his hand away. "I'm sorry if I overstepped."

"No. It's all good. You brought me back to earth, and I needed that." Her head fell into the crook of his neck. "Most journalists just seem to ramp the tension up, but I'm guessing you've calmed a lot of people down."

Well, yes. The best time to interview someone was when the sirens were still flashing and the smoke was still billowing. People often remembered far more in those few precious moments immediately after a tragedy than their minds had any hope of retaining the next morning. But translating those thoughts into actual words was hard to do when their pulses were racing and their minds were in free fall.

She looked down at her phone. "I still can't get a signal. We're going to have to head back up the main road."

His fingers ran gently over the back of her head. "Just rest for a moment, and when you feel up to it, we'll get back in the car and I'll drive until you find a signal."

Her hair brushed against his jaw, filling his head with the scent of sunshine and cinnamon.

He closed his eyes. Yes, he'd hugged victims before, or at least squeezed them comfortingly on the shoulder, but he'd felt nothing like this, never anything like this before. He'd never swept someone up into his arms and felt something inside him reach out for her. And thought he'd felt her reaching back.

"I still feel like my brain is foggy," she murmured, "and I'm only half-awake."

"You're coming out of shock."

"Did I really see my name?"

"Yes, I'm afraid so."

Her fingers squeezed his so hard it almost hurt. "Has the Raincoat Killer ever done anything like this before?"

"No," he said simply. She was still looking at him. A question hovered in her eyes. As a reporter he knew that was all he should say if there was even a chance of interviewing her. But as a man, how could he leave her to process this alone? He took a deep breath. "Okay, I have a theory. It's just a hunch. But if I had to guess, I'd say the killer followed your brother here. Like you say, he's probably not an islander so didn't know where you lived. Maybe McCarthy surprised him. But if it is the Raincoat Killer, he's never killed a man before, or a senior citizen—not that we know of, at least—and he's never tried sending a message." That was the kindest way he could think of putting it. The last scraps of hope he'd had that she wasn't somehow involved in this were quickly disappearing. "You haven't actually been alone since the ferry. You've always had me, or your brother, or the police nearby. So this may be the only way he knew how to get to you."

She pressed her palms into her knees. "Okay, I think I'm good to go again. But if you could drive, that would be great."

A flurry of white fur burst out of the forest. Harry charged toward them, his tail wagging furiously. He launched himself at Meg, his oversized paws landing on her knees, practically pushing her back into the steps. She smiled sadly and rubbed her hand over his head. "Well, Harry. I guess you're coming back home with us now—" She gasped. Then she pressed something into Jack's hand. "Harry had this in his mouth."

It was a strip of waterproof orange fabric.

The rain arrived just before ten, denting the muddy ground at the side of the highway and clattering on the roofs of the vehicles. Jack sat in the backseat of a police car, with his legs hanging out the open door and his boots planted firmly in the mud. Blue-and-red lights swirled through the night air and cut across the ground in front of him.

They'd only needed to drive a few minutes down the road before Meg's phone had found a signal, and then it was only fifteen after that before the authorities had arrived in an impressive phalanx of four police cars, two paramedics and a fire truck. Two cop cars and a paramedic had parked around Meg's hatchback. The rest had carried on to McCarthy's farm, the final vehicle stopping to loop crime-scene warnings around the front of the old man's driveway.

Which is where, Jack thought, *I should be now. At the crime scene. Taking notes. Asking questions. Observing as the cops take down McCarthy's body and searching the scene for clues. That's where I belong.*

But instead Officer Burne had ushered Jack over to his cop car the moment he arrived, ordered him to sit tight and wait for someone to come over and question him. Frustration burned inside him. Wasn't he the same guy some of these very same cops had been pestering with questions just a few hours earlier? Hadn't anyone realized he might actually be able to help them? But barring him from the crime scene wasn't even the worst part. The cops had also separated him from Meg.

He glanced through the dark sheet of rain to where she now sat, curled up in the back of a paramedic's van. A heavy blanket hung around her shoulders. Emergency lights washed over her face, highlighting the lines of her cheeks and deepening her almond-shaped eyes. A blonde, square-jawed officer in a neon-yellow slicker, handed her something in a foam cup and then asked her a question Jack couldn't hear. She was the same officer who'd ushered Meg away from Jack the moment she and officer Burne had pulled up. He hadn't gotten her name.

Another man was standing on Meg's other side. Young, with a trim red beard and civilian clothes, but the cocky stance of someone who was used to being listened to. He'd pulled up in a rental car a few moments after Officer Burne and the blonde cop had arrived. Seemed a bit young for a plain-clothes detective.

Jack's reporter's brain reminded him that separating witnesses before taking their statements was often standard in cases as serious as homicide. But his heart fought back hard against the thought with every thundering beat. Meg had just had the scare of her life. She needed the support of a friend by her side.

The man with the red beard led Meg to her car and helped her in the passenger side. Then he climbed in the driver's side.

Jack stood, but had barely taken a step when he felt a hand on his shoulder.

"I'm afraid I have to ask you to wait in my car, Mr. Brooks." It was Officer Burne. The man's face was shrouded in the unbelievably bright yellow hood of official police rain gear. But somehow water still ran from his mustache. "Someone will be over to take your statement shortly."

Shortly? He clenched his fists together at his side and tried to force the irritation out of his voice. "But it looks like Ms. Duff's car is leaving, and I'm staying with her and her brother, Benji."

"Someone will make sure you are escorted back to your lodgings, after an officer has taken your statement." The officer faked a smile.

Jack eyed the man's artificial smile and matched it with a professional one of his own. What on earth had happened? How was this the same man whom he'd met feeding a dog in a diner that afternoon? "I understand, sir." Was *sir* too formal? Oh well. If so, Burne had started it. "May I at least retrieve my belongings from the front seat?"

"Just sit tight." Burne patted the roof of the cop car. "I'll make sure you get them before the car leaves."

"If I may ask, who's the young man driving the car?"

"Oh, just my son, Malcolm. Big-city Toronto boy like you. Cop on the Toronto force." He chuckled and seemed to unbend a bit. "Drove by, saw the commotion and thought he might as well stop to help his old man." He sauntered off. "Recognized Meg, offered to help drive her home."

Jack watched as he walked over to the car, had a

quick word with the occupants and then returned with Jack's bag.

"Here you go. Shouldn't be much longer until we get to you now."

Meg's car pulled away. She glanced back over her shoulder. He waved. She didn't seem to notice. He sighed, leaned back and looked up at the ceiling.

Well, Lord. This situation is a total dog's dinner bowl of a mess. I'm glad You know what's going on, because I'm so lost for words it ain't funny. Am I missing something I should be seeing?

A tinny song rumbled from inside his bag. He reached in and dug for his phone. The ringing stopped. He glanced at the screen. He'd missed a call from his friend Simon. No, scratch that, scrolling up the screen, it looked as though he'd missed eight calls from Simon. What?

There was only one voicemail. "Hey, Jack, it's Simon. Call me when you can."

The twenty-five-year-old social worker spent his nights walking the streets of Toronto, helping runaways, prostitutes and drug addicts find the life-changing care, respect and dignity needed to help them turn their lives around. A good friend and a fellow member of a Jack's Bible study, Simon was a fellow warrior on the side of all that was right and good. Jack had grown to esteem him as a brother. They were close—but not "talk on the phone every day" close. Why would Simon be calling so persistently?

Only one way to find out. And besides, talking to a solid friend of the faith is exactly what I need to calm myself down.

There was only half a bar on his phone, but when he dialed the number, Simon answered on the first ring.

"Hey, man!" Jack said. A chuckle rumbled through his voice. "Either you sat on your phone and it started dialing random numbers, or you're in one big hurry to talk to me. Either way, I'm so glad to talk to you."

"Jack?" Simon's voice was grim and worried. There was a catch in the back of his throat like a man calling to report news so bad he was struggling to digest it himself. "Where are you now? Is everything okay?" He paused. Then his voice dropped so low Jack could barely hear it. "Are you alone?"

The social worker's words hit Jack's guts like a handful of stones.

"Yeah. I mean, I'm sitting in the back of a cop car waiting to give a statement." He forced a chuckle. Simon didn't laugh back. "But I'm good, and pretty much alone. Why?"

Simon took a deep breath. The phone line crackled.

"Come on, man, I barely have a signal, and I'm

exhausted. Whatever it is, just tell me. Believe it or not, I already confronted a serial killer today. Plus, I just got locked in a garage with a corpse. Nothing you say could possibly be worse than that."

Another pause. Then Simon spoke like a man being strangled. "I don't want to upset you. But I heard something on the streets tonight, and just felt that I had to call and tell you...."

"Yeah?" The rocks in Jack's gut grew heavier.

"I don't know if you're getting much news up where you are, but the local outlets here just started reporting the chief of police is going to call a press conference tomorrow, to update the public on information about the so-called Raincoat Killer...."

Okay, well, that was a good thing. Not surprising, considering the attack on Meg and the death of McCarthy.

"Rumor is he's going to announce the police are naming a 'person of interest' in the case. Now, you know as well as I do that a person of interest is not an official suspect. No warrants are being issued. It's just someone the police are hoping to talk to."

From his work with those who were hurting, Simon knew way more persons of interest than any sane man should.

"Yeah," Jack said. "Because official suspects tend to lawyer up and refuse to be questioned. But announcing someone is a person of interest is still one of the ways cops put pressure on people. Especially when they don't have enough hard evidence to press charges, so hope to trap them into admitting they either committed the crime or know who did. Either that or they think this guy's hiding some key information—"

"Jack? I'm pretty sure it's gonna be you."

The phone slipped in Jack's fingers. The Toronto police were going to name him a person of interest in the Raincoat Killer case? Why? Because he'd been so insistent in convincing people the crimes were the work of a serial killer, they now thought it was him? He tightened his grasp on the phone and forced it back to his ear. His heartbeat grew so loud it nearly drowned out the world around him.

"But that's ridiculous!" he was shouting. Shouting in a cop car, at a crime scene. Burne's head spun toward him. He swallowed hard, forcing his voice back down. "I'm the one who tried to convince the world there was a serial killer on the loose. If it was me, why would I do that?" But even as he said the words he knew the answer. Serial killers were sociopaths and narcissists. They craved attention.

"Look, the announcement won't be until sometime tomorrow. And again, I don't know anything officially." Simon's words came out quickly. "I just heard some cops talking loudly and drunkenly in a back alley behind a bar. They were spouting off nonsense about how some hotshot reporter had angered the chief by trying to make him look like an idiot, and how 'crime-writer boy' was going to get his comeuppance at tomorrow's press conference."

Which wasn't shocking. One of the main alleys Simon walked on his nightly prayer and rescue walks was often used as a smoking hole for a tiny minority of officers who let off steam after work by indulging in their own vices. Simon once admitted he walked that alley purposefully, praying for them.

"Now, if they do, just go in for questioning right away." Simon was in full-on social-worker mode now. "Just be polite, answer their questions and remember you're under no obligation to tell them anything."

Unless they were so furious at his meddling in their investigation they'd actually figured out some way to arrest him. "Okay, brother."

"Keep the faith. I'll be praying."

"Thanks. Me too."

He hung up.

"Mr. Brooks!" Burne called. "We're ready for you."

Jack felt a wave of trepidation wash over him. Was *he* ready for *them?*

TEN

Morning sun streamed through Meg's kitchen window and over the intricately laid fruit and pastry tray. Everything was ready for her meeting with Rachel and the wedding party. She'd sent Benji jogging down to the bakery to pick up an assortment. He really was an amazing brother, even if he did need constant reminding not to leave his dishes under the couch or toss muddy clothes in on top of the clean laundry. Benji and Harry had driven down to the waterfront to open the sports-equipment shop. A thin layer of makeup had been enough to cover the few bruises left from her ordeal yesterday, but she'd tied a delicate silk scarf over the top just in case they showed through.

Jack had yet to make an appearance.

A pair of muddy boots were parked on a mat at the top of the stairs. They'd been there when she woke up this morning, serving as the only evidence Jack had slipped back in to Benji's sometime during the night. She'd waited up almost two hours to talk to him before her aching body forced her into bed. What could have possibly kept him out so late? Had he been interviewing cops at the crime scene?

Or was he was avoiding her? Embarrassed at how he'd held her? Uncomfortable knowing how close they'd been?

And just like that she could feel the icy fingers of anxious insecurity begin to tiptoe up her arms. Her fingers gripped the rim of the double sink. She forced a long, deep breath into her lungs and tried to push away the nagging voices of doubt and fear that had whispered in her mind ever since she was a child.

She'd probably made him feel uncomfortable. She'd been so scared she lost her head. Now here she was, glancing at the basement door, waiting for it to open like a crush-struck teenager. Who was she kidding? He was a gorgeous, big-city reporter with the build of an athlete and a daring smile. He probably had a lineup of beautiful, composed, successful women eager to be his wife. What would he ever want with a broken, timid little thing like her?

All he wanted from her was her story. He wanted to interview her. Nothing more.

She gripped the counter so tightly her knuckles ached. Usually a good long walk, a cup of tea and a time of prayer helped center her mind and keep the wolves of doubt and fear at bay. But now those nagging fears had surged back with a vengeance. For a second, she felt almost as shaken and sick as she had the previous night, when they'd found McCarthy's body.

Yet for a moment she'd felt her heartbeat still when Jack held her. When her legs were about to give way, he'd wrapped his arms around her. When she felt fear filling her mind, he'd lifted her into his arms and run his fingers down her curve of her back. He'd made her feel safe. Surely there'd been more to it than his simply hoping she'd give in to that interview?

She blinked hard and stepped back from the counter. No, she was not going to let herself think this way. They'd been in a terrifying, unreal situation and he'd stepped up to help her. Twice now he'd been her hero in a crisis. But he'd made it clear from the beginning, he was only here because had a job to do.

And she still wasn't about to give him that interview.

There was a hard, rhythmic knock on the front door. She opened the door and froze, as suddenly long-past memories from the girl she'd been at seventeen threatened to flood over the threshold.

A mop of chestnut curls. A roguish grin curving an oversized mouth as Chris Quay leaned into the doorway. *"Hey, cutie. Is your brother ready to hit the snow?"*

Oh, how young she'd been that day. How infatuated she'd been with a boy that her brother had no business going snowmobiling with. How unprepared she'd been to face the cold, hard truth that sometimes life was brutally cut short.

"Hello? Ms. Duff?"

She blinked. The fourteen-year-old memory of Chris faded from her mind, replaced with the very real sight of Chris's thinner, paler and far more timid cousin, Wesley, standing on her doorstep.

"Please, Wesley, call me Meg." She stepped back and beamed a warm smile over the rest of the wedding party. "Welcome, everyone. Please, come in and help yourself. There is fresh coffee in the pot. The wedding decorations and place settings are laid out in the next room, whenever you'd like to head in and take a look."

Wesley bobbed his head. "Thank you for fitting us in this morning." The young groom pushed his glasses up the bridge of his nose and smiled weakly. It was hard to believe this boy of barely twenty-one was just a day away from making the biggest commitment of his life.

"Oh, it's no problem. Really. This is your wedding weekend, and it's my job to make it run as smoothly as possible. I'm here for whatever you need."

"Which is precisely what I told him." Rachel wrapped a protective arm around her fiancé's waist. Her other hand brushed against the back of his neck, in a gesture that was both intimate and possessive, as if the girl who'd once been so desperately lacking in love had now had grown into a young woman determined to clutch on to it for all she was worth.

It was almost hard to believe the sulky teenager who'd slunk into the corner of Meg's Sunday-school class years ago was now the willowy and poised bride standing in front of her. Blond hair cascaded down the bride's back. A focus glinted in her eyes, while her delicate floral sundress did little to hide the sinewy strength of a dancer's frame. With her mother deceased, and a father who had abandoned her as a child, the bride had decided to walk herself down the aisle tomorrow. Looking at her, Meg was unsurprised by the decision. Clearly this was a woman who had learned to stand on her own.

Rachel let go of Wesley, then reached out and gave Meg the kind of artificial embrace designated to keep as much distance as possible between yourself and the person you were hugging. Meg felt the corners of her own smile tighten. Funny how being around some people had the ability to suddenly remind her of exactly what it had been like to be a small, mousy teenager in a class full of flashy beauty queens. Which was why she was so well suited to her job where she had to help other women feel beloved, confident and beautiful. She knew just how to encourage a shy bride into confidence—a part of her work that she loved. Brides like Rachel, on the other hand, set her teeth on edge.

Rachel's eyes ran critically over the pastries. Then she took Wesley by the hand and led him through to where Meg had laid out the place settings and decorations, going over every silk flower and trimming like it held some vital significance. The dress fitting on the mainland yesterday had been frenetic and demanding. Rachel had been sullen and demanded too many last-minute alterations while her maid of honor, Fiona, hung by the wall, too intimidated to speak. Definitely the worst fitting of Meg's career. Then Rachel had become all girly and giggly when the boys had shown up two hours later, dragging the other three around the ferry to take endless cell phone pictures.

Fiona was a year younger than the bride, with delicate features dwarfed by huge, owl-like glasses. She hovered over the fruit tray for a moment, before squeaking out a question about the location of the washroom, and disappearing down the hall toward it.

Which left Meg alone with the large, unsmiling bulk, which was the best man, Duncan. It was rare she had such an instant dislike as she did for Mr. Kitts. The bald geography doctoral student apparently spent most of his time far up North in the frozen tundra, and had only returned to civilization two weeks ago, which might explain his chilly personality. Duncan had started off on the wrong foot at the ferry docks by brushing up against Meg and slurring something in her ear about her giving him a private tour of the island later. When she looked him straight in the eye and politely refused, he'd shot her a poisonous look. Now he was standing in her kitchen, clutching a mug of coffee in his giant hands so tightly she half expected the china to shatter. Just one more reason why she'd be thrilled when this wedding was over tomorrow.

Still, she was a professional, with a job to do. She picked up the pastry tray and tilted it toward him. "So, how do you know Wesley?"

He glanced at the food tray but didn't touch it. "Through Rachel."

"Oh, and how do you know Rachel?"

"Partying."

They met at a party? Or they liked to go "partying" together? She hoped it wasn't slang for drinking and drugs. The young couple already seemed to have enough problems without adding substance abuse into the mix. "You're studying geography, right? Postgrad?"

His large shoulders rose and fell. She'd take that as a yes. Then he reached into his pocket and pulled out his phone.

She set the tray back down and let out a sigh. Guess that meant this conversation was over. Fiona still hadn't returned from the washroom and Rachel was now taking pictures of the reception decorations on her phone. Wesley stood by the front window. A dark blue ribbon twisted through his fingers.

"I'll be making bows with those to decorate the wrought-iron staircase at the pavilion," she said as she walked over to him. "You know both the rehearsal dinner tonight and reception tomorrow are being held on the second floor, right?" Which, as she said it, seemed like an odd thing to tell a groom the day before his wedding. Still, he wouldn't be the first groom she'd met whose entire role had begun and ended at "show up." "The view of the lake is amazing."

Wesley brushed a mop of dusty brown hair from his face. It fell back. "Thank you for doing all this."

"You're very welcome." She smiled. "I love planning beautiful events for people, and the pavilion is one of my favorite spots on the island."

Wesley's Adam's apple bobbed. "Rachel picked it for her grandmother, because her grandfather built it. It's all..." He glanced back down at the ribbon in his fingers. "Unreal, you know? I guess until I saw all the work you and Rachel had put into it, it hadn't sunk in that we were really doing this thing tomorrow. I'm really happy to be with Rachel. It's just, when I agreed to get married so her grandma would let us move to London together, I guess I didn't imagine it would turn into something this big."

Meg nodded slowly. He definitely wasn't the first person to admit to cold feet in the hours before his wedding. Her hand slid over his shoulder. It was bony. "That's perfectly normal. A lot of people feel that way before they get married. It's a big, lifelong commitment you're making."

Would Wesley even be considering getting married this young if he wasn't moving to England? As she seemed to remember hearing, he'd been accepted to a prestigious history program there almost a year ago, which had left Rachel to claw and fight through auditions to gain a coveted dance spot at a London dance institution so that they had a reason to move there together. Only to then have her grandmother decree the only way Rachel would chase a young man halfway across the world would be as his wife.

"I was sorry to hear about your parents," she added.

His shoulders shook slightly under her palm. He looked up. "Thanks. You know it was cancer, right? Diagnosed a year apart. Died three months apart. Rachel says it's kind of romantic in a way."

Only if you found romance in tragedies. Rachel was watching them from the other room. Meg pulled her hand away.

"Can I ask you something?" Wesley's words came out in a rush. He looked up at her. "That tree on the road, the one with all the ribbons? Is that where my cousin died?"

Sudden tears rushed to her eyes. "It is. Your cousin, Chris, was quite the athlete and won a lot of awards. In the weeks after the accident, a lot of his peers took the ribbons off their medals and tied them to the tree where he died. Over time it became a tradition that people tied ribbons there in remembrance." She took a deep breath and felt it catch in her lungs. "You're welcome to take a ribbon with you. Maybe you and Rachel can tie one of your wedding ribbons there, as a way to remember him?"

"I can't tell whether or not I remember him." Wesley's voice was so soft she could barely catch the words. "He was my only cousin and I was really young. But I dream about him sometimes. About him dying. For a long time I thought I was going to die at eighteen too…." His voice trailed off. "I'm sorry. I don't know why I just said that."

She blinked hard. "It's okay. I understand." *Oh, Lord, as much as I might hate this wedding, thank*

*You for giving me the chance to talk to Wesley.
Help me know what to say.* "My brother, Benji,
was snowmobiling with your cousin when he died.
I'm sure he'd be happy to talk to you about Chris.
I can bring you all by the store later."

"What store?" Rachel strode across the kitchen.
Her hand reached for Wesley's. "Everything
okay?"

"Absolutely," Meg said. "Wesley and I were just
talking about his cousin, Chris, and I was telling him my brother was snowmobiling with him
the day he died. I suggested you might stop by
my brother's store later today, if you wanted. We
could all meet back at your hotel an hour before
the rehearsal. Benji would probably be more than
happy to talk to you about the accident. He talks
about it a lot, actually, to schools and stuff. Maybe
he could even look over the yacht you rented, and
make sure it's got everything it needs for your
honeymoon."

Wesley glanced at his bride. Rachel frowned
slightly. Her lips pressed together as if she was
looking at something complex and serious that
only she could see. Finally she sighed.

"Yeah." Rachel slid her arm around Wesley's
waist. "Yeah, I can see that's a good idea. Anything to help you feel better about your cousin.
And if our wedding planner thinks we've got time

to squeeze another thing into today, then who am I to argue?"

"Wonderful. I'll give Benji a quick call right now."

Thank You, Lord! After she'd been so worried about arranging a wedding for Chris's cousin, now it looked as though God was actually going to use it for the best. Finally something was beginning to look up.

Jack paced the basement apartment. His eyes darted from the clock on the wall to the phone in his hands. What was taking Vince so long?

He'd called the editor's desk at *Torchlight News* almost six times that morning before he finally managed to reach his boss at a quarter after nine. Vince had answered the phone grumpy, thanks to a delay on his morning commute and a coffee that had grown cold before he'd managed to drink it. When Jack had added to Vince's morning joys with the news that he might be named a person of interest in the Raincoat Killer case, at the police chief's next press conference, Vince had sworn, then apologized and then promised to look into it and call Jack back as soon as he knew something. He'd hung up before Jack could say another word.

That was half an hour ago, which might not seem like a long time from the editor's perspective, but practically felt like a year from where

Jack was standing. The phone began to ring. He hammered on the button so hard he nearly dropped it on the floor. "Yeah, Vince?"

"Hi." The editor sighed, like a man who'd just gone twelve rounds in a boxing ring with an opponent who fought dirty, barely gotten out alive, and then had the match called on a technicality.

"What's the news?"

"The chief's a stupid, arrogant fool with a serious bone to pick about that article you wrote." There was the sound of Vince's office chair squeaking on ancient springs. "Sadly, your source wasn't wrong. The chief is going to name you as a person of interest today. Which is one of the most pigheaded things I've ever heard in my career."

Jack felt the breath leave his lungs. He dropped sideways into a chair. "Wow."

"As you can imagine we had some choice words," Vince said. "Loud ones. Like his calling up my publisher's office and demanding we fire you wasn't enough, now he's got to make life a whole lot harder by dragging your name even further through the mud.

"Of course he doesn't believe you have anything to do with the Rainbow, Raincoat Killer or whatever you're calling him. He doesn't even believe there is a serial killer on the loose. He just thinks some cocky reporter made him and his force look bad by implying they weren't doing their jobs.

Then he gets a call from the provincial police up North, saying you're up there, reporting serial-killer sightings. You know as well as I do, kid, that this chief abuses the whole 'person of interest' thing way too often, just as some way of intimidating people or trying to convince the public the police force is actually doing something."

Jack groaned. Tension was rising through his body, like quick-setting cement, spreading up his back all the way to the nape of his neck. "But he can't name me a person of interest in a series of crimes without admitting there's actually a connection between them. So, if he names me a person of interest in all four murders, basically he's saying he believes that one person was behind them all." *And that this person is me.*

"'Course not." Vince snorted. "He's sticking to his guns on saying that there's no serial killer. He's just now naming you as a person of interest in the crime of intentionally creating a big, public nuisance and scaring the good people of this city by inventing an imaginary serial killer.

"See, what you gotta realize, Jacky, my boy, is that when you walked into that police station up there and reported knowledge of a Toronto-based serial killer, the chief's problem suddenly went from having one Toronto reporter yapping his gums to having police officers from another part of the province calling him up asking questions. That freaked the chief so bad he saw red. What happens to his career if the police up North believe you and not him? What if the police up there leak this story to the national press? You think he wants someone in government calling up to ask him what kind of police service he's running in Toronto? So, yeah. He's going to act fast and throw the one thorn-in-his-side reporter who started this mess under the biggest bus he can find. 'Course I told him that if his own officers were gonna get drunk and run their mouths off, maybe he should be taking a better look at his own house instead of chucking mud at mine." Vince chuckled. Jack didn't.

"Please just tell me we're not going to back down from this story," Jack said. "It doesn't matter what the chief of police's detectives are telling him—they're wrong. There *is* a serial killer on the loose and people are going to keep dying until he's behind bars. A man was killed here last night. A woman was strangled nearly to death on the ferry before being dumped overboard, and she would've drowned if I wasn't there—"

"And I presume you're about to send me a tight little interview with this woman detailing every single aspect of your story?" Vince asked. "And then you're going to assure me, on every remaining shred of your journalistic integrity, that she's not going to recant when the Toronto police, the provincial police, the Mounties, her neighbors and the entire might of the national press show up on her doorstep wanting to hear the story for themselves. Right?"

Jack clenched his jaw and glanced at the ceiling. "What if she doesn't want to be interviewed and wants me to keep her name out of the press? What if I can figure out who the killer is and bring him to justice without involving her?"

"Do you even hear yourself?" Vince sighed. "Look, I'm down here in the trenches, mud up to my elbows, fighting for my star reporter against a police chief who wants to strangle him, and my own publisher who's ready to throw him out the door to the waiting mob. Today's Friday. I can give you till Monday, that's it. Go, get me an interview with the girl. Get it today. Make it so good it shines like the blinding glare of polished gold. Otherwise there's gonna be nothing I can do."

ELEVEN

Meg closed the front door and had just begun to breathe a sigh of relief at the sight of the wedding party heading down the driveway when she heard the basement door open. She turned. The door to Benji's lair was open a crack. But no one came through.

"Hello? Jack?" Meg crossed through the kitchen. "Come on up. I'm sorry, I guess I should have mentioned I was having clients over. I hope you didn't feel you had to hide down there until they were done." She reached for the door. "But they are gone now and they've left plenty of food behind if you're hungry."

She opened the door. Jack was standing partway down the steps, as if debating whether he wanted to head up the stairs or down. He had a voice recorder and a notebook in his hand.

"Good morning," he said softly. "Did you sleep well?" He ran the back of his hand down, along his unshaved jawline. "You look a lot better rested than I feel right now."

Her cheeks flushed. "Yes, and thank you. I was hoping to stay up until you got back. But sleep got the better of me."

"Well, yesterday was a pretty overwhelming day." He paused. Uncertainty flickered in the depths of his eyes. "I saw Officer Burne's son gave you a ride home. Did it go okay?"

"Malcolm? Yeah, of course. He's a really good guy. Though I'm not sure what I think of his wife's plan to start a wedding business up here and give me more competition."

He nodded slowly as if he was mentally jotting the words down on some notepad. If he was actually about to ask her if she thought Malcolm could be the Raincoat Killer, she'd probably laugh in his face.

He didn't. "Did you manage to look up those names in your database for me?"

She watched his lips as they moved. He had a strong mouth. Determined. She leaned her head back against the wall and paused for a moment, soaking in the solid, reliable feeling of concrete and plaster behind her. "No. I'm sorry. Not yet. Would you like me to now?"

"Sure. Thanks." His mouth melted into an easy, relaxed smile that sent butterflies dancing through her chest. *Come on, Meg. Get a hold of yourself.*

No matter how close she'd felt to him when their lives were in danger last night, now it was time for both of them to get back to reality.

He followed her through the kitchen and past the remains of the brunch, pausing only to pour himself black coffee from the pot. The air in her office was cool. The space was tidy, with a small, spotless desk and two soft beige chairs with lilac throw pillows. She slid into her desk chair and opened her laptop. It hummed softly to life.

His arm brushed against her shoulder as Jack braced his hand on the desk and leaned in toward the screen. "What kind of records do you keep?"

"Really basic ones." She opened her database. "Names of the wedding party. Budgets. Contact details. Nothing about their personal histories. What were the names of the victims again?"

"Krista Hooper. She's the one who interrupted a robbery in her dorm room three months ago. Then Eliza Penn, who died two months ago in an apparent hit-and-run. Finally Shelly Day, who was stabbed two weeks ago."

"I don't recognize any of the names, but I will try them. Maybe they were in a wedding party or called me for a quote."

"You save those names too?"

She glanced up at him and smiled. "I save everything." She entered the names. No results. She tried just the last names. Still no results. She sat back. "I'm sorry, I don't have any record of having contact with any of them."

He pushed both hands up through his hair, pressed his fingers into his head and sighed.

"Hey, you okay?" She leaned toward him. "You seem disappointed. Surely the fact that none of my clients are connected to a serial killer is a good thing, right?"

He didn't meet her eye. "Would it be okay if I just scrolled through all the names myself? Just in case I see someone I recognize, or something jumps out at me?"

"Sure, as long as it's just names. Don't go clicking through to anyone's bank details or dress measurements."

He chuckled. "Deal."

She turned the screen toward him. He picked up her laptop, leaned back against the desk and scrolled. For several minutes, he looked through names in silence, staring at each one in turn, as if seeing the right combination of letters might unlock something locked inside memory. His brow furrowed.

"Wesley Tens. Would be related to Carol Tens? The aunt of Chris Quay, who was in an accident with your brother?"

She blinked. "How on earth would you know that?" She hadn't even remembered Chris's cousin's last name until she'd seen Wesley in person.

"Yes, Wesley is Chris's younger cousin. He was just here a few minutes ago. You met him yesterday after we left the diner. But his mother, Carol, passed away from cancer not that long ago."

"Carol Tens wrote an open letter to the national press pushing for stronger helmet laws. She claimed Chris's death caused her son to have nightmares and behavioral problems in school. Several newspapers still have it online in their archives. This was a few years ago." He didn't meet her eye. "I made a point of reading pretty much everything I could find online about your brother's accident last night and this morning. Couldn't really sleep."

She winced. How many articles on her brother's crash were still floating around online, for anyone to find, with just a simple internet search? How many of those were even accurate?

"Well, you can't believe everything you read online. A lot of the articles they wrote after the accident were nothing but speculation and nonsense. You wouldn't believe the utter garbage that got printed, even after the police determined that Chris was the one driving and Benji was just the passenger."

He set down the laptop. "I asked you yesterday if there was anyone who was on that ferry who had a reason to want to hurt you. You said there wasn't. Now you're telling me that you're arranging a wedding for the cousin of the very kid who died in a wreck involving your brother."

"Now you sound exactly like one of them." She spun her chair toward him so quickly her legs smacked into his. "Yes, the groom who's getting married tomorrow is Chris's cousin, not that he even knew my brother was in the same accident until I just told him today. He was only seven when Chris died. I get the impression the knowledge his cousin died young haunted him on an emotional level. Not that he meticulously memorized the details let alone grew up planning to avenge Chris's death." She could feel the words bubbling through her like a river overflowing its banks. Jack held up a finger to interject. She didn't let him. "Wesley is nothing but a sad, lost kid who's just doing his best to deal with the life he's been given. Plus, he's so scrawny. There's no way he is strong enough to be the man who attacked me on the ferry."

Jack crossed his arms slowly and stood. "Anything else you think I need to know?"

"No. Well, yes." Her heart was racing so hard she could barely think. "If you're going to investigate Wesley, then I might as well tell you that the best man, Duncan, is a huge bear of a man. He definitely has the right build to be the Raincoat Killer. But I don't get the impression he and Wesley are close enough that he'd kill for him.

Besides, he only got back from the Arctic a few days ago. That's three planes and several hours of flying each direction from the previous crime scenes. So unless he somehow managed to pop down from the frozen tundra on weekends just to commit murder, then fly back again, he's not your guy either."

Jack's mouth turned up at the corner. "Well, that should be easy enough to check."

She watched his chest rise and fall, just inches away from her own. "I'm sorry if I sound defensive, but you just reminded me—whether you meant to or not—that all the terrible stories the press wrote about my brother are still floating around the internet, and will be for the rest of his life. Then you followed it up by speculating that same accident might have turned Chris's little cousin into a cold-blooded killer?"

His shoulders stiffened. "I did no such thing. I just asked a question."

"Just like all the other reporters who came around and asked questions about what happened after Chris and Benji's accident. If word gets out that the Raincoat Killer is targeting me, it's just going to happen all over again. Gossip journalists and bloggers are going to pick me apart under the microscope. Guessing what might be wrong with me. Guessing what I might have done to deserve getting attacked. Guessing how I might feel or how I might be affected. Without actually having a clue what it's like."

"Then why don't you tell them?" Jack picked up his voice recorder. It spun between his fingers. "I won't lie to you. I think the national press is going to eventually come knocking on your door, asking about what happened to you and to Mr. McCarthy." His voice softened. "I'm sorry, Meg, but you can't hide from something like this. Stories like these have a way of coming out. So, isn't it better coming from you?"

Sudden tears pushed to the edges of her eyelids. She bit her lower lip and blinked them back. "You don't understand, Jack."

"Then tell me." He set the recorder on the table and reached for her hand. "Has it ever crossed your mind that your story could help other people?" he asked. "Every time I run an interview with someone who's been through a major tragedy, my email is swamped with letters from readers, saying, 'Thank you for giving a voice to how I feel! Thank you for letting me know I'm not alone!' That's the reason I do what I do. When you give someone the chance to tell his story, it can transform his tragedy into something that changes other people's lives."

She looked down at this hand. Did he have any idea how much she wanted to take it? Did he know how desperately she wanted to just step into his

chest and let him wrap his arms around her in a
hug as he had done last night? But she couldn't.
This wasn't a man looking to hold her. This was
a man looking to take what she wasn't willing to
give.

"Can you honestly tell me that if you interview me, if you write a newspaper article, telling the world that I was targeted by the Raincoat
Killer, I'm not going to have brides second-guessing whether they still want me as their wedding
planner?"

He pulled his hand away. "You know I can't
guarantee that."

He ran his hand over the back of his neck. She
gripped the chair to keep from reaching for him.

"I'm sorry," she said. "Maybe I can't control
what other people are going to write about me.
And maybe if I went around talking to every person who asked about my personal life, like Benji
does, I'd be as confident as he is answering questions about his accident. But I'm not going to risk
wrecking my life any further by accidentally blurting out something personal to a reporter who's
then going to put it in print, where people can see
it and use it against me.

"You think you know what happened that
night, because you talked to my brother about
the accident, and stayed up late reading a lot of
newspaper articles. But I guarantee you don't

know the whole story about Benji and Chris. That's my point. No one does."

Jack stared down at the lukewarm sludge in his cup. He tried to swirl it without spilling any onto his hands. Coffee grains stuck to the side. Meg had been kind enough to drop him off at the police station without asking him why. He wasn't sure if that was a good thing or a bad thing. Officer Burne hadn't even raised an eyebrow when Jack walked into the station, but simply ushered him into an interview room and told him to help himself to coffee.

The coffee now churned inside Jack's gut. It hadn't felt this bad when he sat in Vince's office two days ago and had been asked to consider taking a leave of absence. No, at that time he'd felt indignant, determined, self-righteous even.

But now that strong grip he'd had on his emotions had gotten all muddled up somehow, into a mess of uncertainty and doubt.

He'd found the news story that could save his career. But if he wrote it, Meg would never forgive him. Somehow the thought of upsetting her like that was as uncomfortable as a mosquito bite under his skin he didn't know how to scratch. But if he had been willing to throw his career away and walk away from his story, what difference would it even make? He wasn't the kind of man she'd ever want to have a future with.

Oh, Lord, help me have my head on straight and keep my emotions in check.

Officer Burne set a voice recorder on the table in front of Jack and sat down.

"So, Mr. Brooks. What brings you in this morning?" He didn't smile.

Jack forced his best professional smile on his face. "Well, Officer, I'm guessing you heard that I was named a person of interest in a case in Toronto?"

The officer nodded. "Yup. We did."

"So I'm just checking in with my closest police station and letting them know where I am, should anyone have any more questions for me. The Toronto police haven't contacted me. I'm not sure if they're planning on sending someone up here to question me, or if they want you to question me, or what they're going to do."

A wane smile crossed the officer's face. If Jack had to guess, he hadn't wanted this whole mess landing in his police station any more than Jack wanted it to be there.

Jack took a deep breath. "Would you like me to go over my story again from the beginning? How I first covered the deaths of Krista, Eliza and Shelly, and why I concluded we were looking at the work of a serial killer? How I confronted the Raincoat

Killer when he tried to kill Ms. Duff on the ferry? My account of Mr. McCarthy's murder?"

"Would you be telling me anything significantly different from the last time you told me those stories?"

"No, sir."

Burne leaned over and switched off the recorder. Then he loosened his top button, and leaned his arms on the table. "Look, Jack. Can I call you Jack?"

He nodded. Well, so much for the formalities.

"You seem like a nice enough guy," Burne said. "My gut tells me you believe you're telling the truth. Certainly the truth as you know it. So let me tell you where I'm coming from. I see Meg Duff, a girl I've known practically since she was born, utterly terrified because someone attacked her on the ferry, and she introduces you as her noble defender. You tell me this big story about how she's just the latest victim of a serial killer, and I believe you.

"Then I get home and tell the whole story to my son, Malcolm, who's just arrived up from the Toronto force, and he laughs at me! My son tells me you're probably the same kooky reporter who's got his chief of police all worked up by running around telling some story in the press about a serial killer who only exists in your imagination." He sat back. "So you can imagine how I'm feeling when my own son starts asking me questions. Like, did anyone actually see you and the Raincoat Killer together on this ferry? Is it possible you put on a raincoat, knocked Meg overboard, then jumped in to save her?" He tilted his chair back and eyed Jack. "And while my gut tells me that's not what happened, I can't prove it."

Jack couldn't believe what he was hearing. "What about McCarthy's murder?"

"Which just so happens to look exactly like a suicide?"

"Surely once you get a crime-scene investigator to examine the bruise patterns—"

"You think a town this small is going to use up their resources to call in experts from the mainland, just in case a supposed serial killer who, by your own claims, has only ever gone after beautiful young women suddenly decided to fake a miserable old man's suicide? Do you honestly think that's how things work around here? You should know I did actually convince Toronto police to send up one of their detectives to consult on our investigation. But I had to stick my own neck pretty far out to make it happen. He arrives later this afternoon. I'm hoping I won't have to sit there and listen to him tell me that we were all fooled by a hoax."

Jack clenched his jaw so tightly the muscles ached. He should probably be thankful Officer

Burne was being honest with him, and still taking things this seriously. But it didn't take away the sting of being called a liar. "Both Meg and I saw someone at McCarthy's farm."

Burne nodded. "Yup, you both say you did. But unfortunately all she saw was the shadowy figure in a hood. Hardly credible."

"There's the scrap of orange fabric…."

"Which is so generic it could've come from anywhere."

"There was a handwritten sign, on the man's body, with Meg's name on it! You're trying to tell me that doesn't count as some pretty heavy-duty evidence?"

"We couldn't find it, Jack!" The officer leaned forward. His eyes were as unflinching as steel. "There was no note. Not when we got there. Am I supposed to believe someone stuck a note on that body just for you and Meg to see, and then took it down after you left the crime scene but before we got there? Trust me, we went over every inch of that place and every inch of that body. Not a single one of my officers saw any evidence of that sign."

TWELVE

Benji was waiting outside the police station, leaning up against his pickup truck with a takeaway coffee cup in each hand, when Jack finally emerged. "Hey." He nodded to Jack, then walked over and handed him a cup. "When I heard you were hanging out here, I figured you could use one of these."

Jack took a sip. The coffee was still hot. "Thank you."

"No problem. The stuff they give you in there is swill."

That wasn't a half-bad word for it. "Hey, you don't happen to know of any criminal masterminds who hang out on the island, do you?"

Benji snorted so hard he nearly spit coffee. "Nah. Just a few drunken idiots. Meg tell you about Kenny and Stuart Smythe?"

"Teenaged brothers? Yeah, I already had the privilege of meeting them."

"Well, sorry, I think that's the worst we've got."

Benji chuckled to himself. "Okay, now I've got to head back to the store. Harry probably thinks I left him in charge. You want a ride?"

"Yeah. Thanks." Not that Jack had any clue what he was going to do next, just that it didn't involve hanging around the police station. He took another sip of coffee. Tasted like a "double double." Two cream and two sugar. Whole lot heartier than his usual straight black. His gut was thankful for it. "You been waiting long?"

"Not long." Benji got into his truck. Jack followed. The vehicle was huge, black and purred like a kitten. He couldn't help noticing Benji waited until Jack had done up his seat belt before putting it into drive.

"How'd you know I was—"

"A 'person of interest' in a dastardly crime?" He eyed Jack's face, then guffawed. "A buddy of mine who's a cop dropped in this morning and told me."

"Does Meg know?"

"Nope." He turned his eyes back to the road. "'Cause I haven't heard from her today, and I'm pretty sure if she found out, she'd call me first. But take my advice, and make sure she hears it from you. If she gets the news from someone else, it won't go down so well."

"And you're okay with it?"

"Let's say I'm willing to listen. As you know, I was once a person of interest in the unlawful vehicular manslaughter of Chris Quay. Or some such. Don't really remember the details of what they wanted to charge me with. I was still in a coma at the time." He eased the truck onto the rural highway. "We got about twenty minutes till I reach the shop. So, how about you tell me what I need to know?"

Fair enough. Jack started way back at the beginning. Over twelve years of crime reporting, developing the instincts that made him look for possible connections. Three murders within three months. All young women. All by someone with an orange raincoat.

"I'm not the only one who thought this was the work of a serial killer. A lot of ordinary cops do too." Jack drained his coffee. "You should have heard some of the crime-scene theories and gossip I was privy to. It's not like I was just making up a story off the top of my head. But I can't ethically report anything I see or hear off the record. As a journalist, I can report nothing but the facts of the cases, and the statements made by the official spokespeople. And the official spokespeople keep saying I'm nuts.

"But to be fair, they have their reasons. Every single murder was committed in a drastically different way, which is practically unheard of in serial killings. Raincoats are hardly rare in Canada this time of year. Plus, there were completely conflicting accounts on how big the killer was. Witness from one crime said he was small, another said he was big."

The road curved sharply to the right. Trees filed past the window on one side, water on the other. Jack stared into his cup. "Maybe I was wrong. Maybe I shouldn't have pushed my editor into running that story. But I was frustrated. Really frustrated. Women were dying. I guess I thought if I published the story, then it would force the police to do something. That if I stuck my neck out, investigators would take a harder look at the cases and find a connection that could lead to the killer, or politicians would put pressure on the police to dig deeper. I don't know. I thought I was fighting for justice. Instead the chief of police himself denounces me and my publisher wants to fire me. My editor is trying to protect me, but there's only so much he can do. He told me to use up some vacation days and take a break while things died down."

"But you didn't do that," Benji said.

Jack barked out a laugh. "Of course not. There were Manitoulin Island ferry schedules near all three crime scenes. The final one had yesterday afternoon's ferry circled. There was a flyer for your sister's wedding business at the last crime scene too. So I woke up yesterday morning with no job to go to and decided to hop a bus up here to check out the ferry. Then I decided I might as well catch the ferry and visit the island for a couple of days. I saw your sister on the boat and decided to go over and talk to her." He crumpled the cup and then shoved it back in the cup holder. "Guess you could say I haven't exactly been planning all this through thoughtfully. I'm not like Meg with her meticulous spreadsheets. Instead I've just been running around like a headless chicken, chasing my instincts."

The truck stopped. Jack looked up. They were in a small parking lot behind a row of shops.

Benji was looking at him. "So, what are you going to do to change that?"

"I don't know if there's anything I *can* do," Jack said. "Everything in my gut says the serial killer was one of the hundreds of people on that ferry. But the ferry doesn't keep a passenger list, and I have no idea how many people on that ferry even came from Toronto. In fact, there are only three men who I know for certain came up from southern Ontario yesterday, and Meg seems fully convinced none of them could possibly have committed the Toronto murders."

Benji turned off the engine. "I didn't ask what you could or couldn't do. I asked what you were *going to* do. Sounds like your priority now is getting a story, right? How you going about that?"

Good question. Jack stared at the ceiling. "Well,

if I was back at my desk I'd start by checking to see if Meg was right about that one guy she mentioned having an alibi for the murders. Duncan Kitts—the best man for the wedding she's planning. She didn't say anything directly against him, but I could tell from her expression that she doesn't like him, and that's good enough for me. I'd also try to see what I could find out about the groom, Wesley. Meg said he's related to the young man who was driving the snowmobile during your accident?" Benji nodded. "Plus, I know for sure of one other man from Toronto who was on that ferry and who thinks I'm telling fairy tales—Officer Burne's son, Malcolm. But Meg seems pretty convinced he can't possibly be guilty, so I guess you'd feel the same."

Benji grinned and got out of the truck. "It's like this. A guy comes into my shop last week, convinced a bear shred his campsite. Black bear, he tells me. Or maybe a brown bear. Big, huge bear anyway. Now, I know a thing or two about where he went camping, and honestly, I'm pretty sure he just got spooked by a really fat raccoon." He opened a door and walked through into the back of the sports shop. "But I wasn't there. I don't know for sure. So all I said to him is the exact same thing I'm going to say to you right now, 'How can I help you fix the problem?'"

Jack followed him into the store. It was the most

amazingly organized clutter he had ever seen. Canoes and paddles hung from the ceiling. Life jackets covered the far wall. Lawn chairs sat in front of a tent that had been set up in the middle of the store. Harry lay on a putting green. Benji nodded to a slim blond behind the counter, then headed for his office. "Now, I've got a place here for you to plug in your laptop, a phone you can use, a fax machine and an internet connection. Help yourself."

"Thank you," Jack said, feeling he was at risk of wearing out the words. There was a clutter of newspaper cutouts taped to the glass wall that divided the office from the rest of the store. Local Youths in Critical Condition After Snowmobile Crash. Snowmobile Safety Questioned After Fatal Accident. His eyes ran over the newsprint images of Benji's and Chris's young, wide-eyed faces. "I'm kind of surprised you'd want to be reminded of this every day."

Benji shrugged. "It's like this. I'm going to remember the accident my whole life. I gain nothing by fighting against what happened. All I can do is learn from it and move on. I've got nothing to hide. It was a terrible thing. I got physical therapy, emotional therapy, spiritual therapy and if I rolled up my pant leg right now, you'd see I've still got the scars. But let me guess, you tried to talk to Meg about it and she shot you down?"

"Yeah. She won't even talk to me about what's happened these past couple of days."

"I'm not surprised. Talking about things frightens her now. I've practically begged Meg to talk to our pastor, a therapist, a doctor, a friend, me." He shrugged. "She won't. And if you try to push her too hard, she'll cut you out completely."

Late-afternoon sunlight spread through the store's front windows and cast long shadows over the floor. The front door chimes jangled. Jack didn't look up. So many people had gone in and out all afternoon that he'd long stopped noticing. When he was sunk deep into research, the rest of the world just faded into the background. Jack ran his hand over the back of his neck. How long had he been at this? Hours. Long enough to call in every favor he could get with every cop on the Toronto force who still believed in him, not to mention every friendly researcher at *Torchlight*. Long enough to have confirmed that even if Duncan, the best man, gave Meg the creeps his Arctic alibi was so solid there was no way he could have killed Krista or Eliza. He'd also discovered that Rachel, the bride, and Fiona, her maid of honor, were in arts programs similar to Krista's, and had even auditioned for some of the same shows—along with hundreds of other women. He couldn't find anything out of the ordinary on Wesley, except a leave of absence from school after the death of his parents. He even looked into Officer Burne's son, Malcolm Burne, who seemed to be a good cop, though with a reputation for being a bit louder and more controlling than situations called for. Jack tried to avoid the temptation of reading what the Toronto press outlets were saying about him, and only partially succeeded. He'd just have to hope that when the investigator arrived from Toronto he'd actually be willing to take the case seriously.

Come on. There had to be something somewhere he was missing. A thread he could pull on. A lead he could chase. Yet every hunch he'd had was coming up dry.

At least he'd been able to get through to his friend Simon, who'd prayed with him on the phone for a good fifteen minutes, before asking Jack to email him any pictures he had of the people connected to the story. Simon had promised to show them around downtown just in case it turned up anything. You didn't survive as a social worker in some of Toronto's roughest neighborhoods without making a few trusted contacts.

Jack rolled his shoulders back and looked up through the clipping-covered office glass, out into the store. That's when he saw her, standing by the front door. Meg had her back to him. Her face was turned toward the dark blue waters outside. The rays of the late afternoon sun silhouetted her slender frame. Her arms slid around her body, fingers brushing the back of her neck. He felt his mouth go dry.

How could someone manage to look so strong and yet so fragile at the same time? She was carrying too many burdens already. He hated the thought of adding even more to her load.

Yet the bottom line was simple. His other research had turned up nothing. He was back to square one, with no other story and nothing else to offer Vince. If he didn't write an article about Meg, he could kiss both his career and reputation goodbye. Which somehow meant convincing her to give him the very thing she was determined not to let him have.

Benji rapped on the divider. "Hey. You still awake in there?"

"Yeah." Jack pressed his fingertips into his temples. "Thanks again for this."

"Any time. I just hope it turned up something helpful." Benji spun a thick key chain around on his fingers. "I'm just about to close up for the day. Meg brought her wedding group by, to get some supplies for their honeymoon yacht. So I'm going to help them run the supplies over and give the boat a quick checkup. As you know, the groom is the cousin of Chris Quay, and Meg thinks it might help if he and I have a chat. Maybe make him feel less nervous about getting married tomorrow."

Jack nodded, even though he felt he was only catching half of what Benji was saying. He glanced past Benji. He couldn't see the women, but Wesley was by the counter, clutching a mass of bags. A large, bald man was standing in the corner near the life jackets, typing on a phone and scowling. Guess that would be Duncan.

"So, you're going to be okay if I leave you here alone for a bit?" Benji asked. "If you want to leave, just pull the door behind you. I've already put the lights on a timer, set the locks and switched on the security cameras."

"Sure thing. Thanks."

"Catch you later." Benji clasped him on the shoulder. Then he disappeared back onto the sales floor. There was a rustle of bags. Muted conversation. A bark. Lights switched. A door slammed. Silence.

Jack unfolded his legs out from under the desk and stood. His whole body ached. The laptop and notes went back into his bag. Then he stepped out of the office and into the empty shop. For a moment he just let himself wander aimlessly, up and down aisles, drinking in the climbing equipment, hiking gear, harnesses and rafts. If it wasn't for the threat of getting the ax on Monday, he could probably have spent hundreds in any one of the aisles without even noticing. He headed into the maze of artificial trees that was the camping section.

"Hey, Jack." He jumped. Meg was sitting in a lawn chair in front of the tent. Lights glowed gently in a fire pit in by her feet.

"Hey." He dropped into the chair beside her. "I thought you'd gone to the yacht with your brother and the others."

She smiled gently. "Benji offered to take them off my hands for a while. I think he could tell I was finding them a bit much." Her ankles crossed gently on the plastic fire pit. She leaned back and looked up. A rainbow parachute stretched across the ceiling above them. "It's an amazing store, isn't it?" She sighed. "I'm so proud of him for building this. Even if it's not always easy."

Jack tried to copy her posture, only to be nearly tossed backward onto the floor. Why most camp-chair makers seemed to think no one over six foot ever went camping was beyond him. "I saw your brother covered his office window with stories about the accident."

"Yeah, he's sort of made it part of his business. He goes everywhere—schools, camps, churches—and talks about sports safety. He's really respected for it. Benji Duff, the sports-safety guru, who nearly died. I'm…I'm the only one who seems to want to forget it."

He watched as she pressed her lips together to hide their trembling. Both his brain and heart were so full of words he could practically feel them fighting inside him to get out. What would happen if he just laid it all out on the line and told her that if she didn't agree to the interview he'd lose his job? She wasn't made of stone. Surely she'd understand. And yet how was that fair of him? How could he possibly ask her to open up her own wounds and pain, just to save him from the mess he'd gotten himself into? *Help me, Lord.* If only she knew how much he understood what she was going through.

He swiveled to face her. "I want to tell you a story. Okay? A story that isn't that easy to tell, and one that I don't tell a lot of people. But I think it might help. All right?" When she nodded, he took a deep breath and let it out again. Where to start? The worst part. Always start at the very worst part. "Years ago, I was suspended from college. Put on academic probation, in fact. I lost editorship of the college paper too."

The smile faded from her face. "What?" Her fingers slid over his arm.

He pulled her hand into his and held it tightly. "I always knew I liked both writing and talking to people. But I couldn't decide between a career in journalism and one in counseling. By my second year, I was editor of the college newspaper and volunteering in student services. I grew really close to this one fellow student. A young woman. I felt sorry for her, because she'd had a rough background. We were never romantically involved." He shook his head. "But if I'm honest, part of me hoped one day we would be."

He loosened his grip on her hand, half expecting her to pull away. But instead she linked her fingers through his. He looked down at the tender, slender hand, wrapped around his calloused one. "She was arrested for stealing and selling student papers. I didn't want to believe she was guilty. So I tried to use my job at the paper to clear her name. I was too close to her. It clouded my judgment. I overlooked information that didn't fit my theory. I tweaked quotes. I let her look at my notes. I leaked off-the-record information that impeded the police investigation." He pulled his hand away from her and stood.

"I told myself that I was doing the right thing and helping her. But basically I was just being young and foolish, not to mention arrogant. I lost my job at the paper and was suspended. By then, I had no choice but to see the truth, and I realized just how badly I'd messed up. I waited out my suspension, went on and graduated. But my reputation never recovered. And if you search my name on the internet today, that will still come up somewhere on the first page. Not the years of respected journalism I did afterward. Not the thousands of good, solid, professional stories I've written. No, as far as the internet is concerned, I'm living forever online as a guy who broke his principles and acted unprofessionally when he was barely more than a teenager in order to protect a girl he had a crush on."

Winsome eyes met his, and a peculiar pain filled his rib cage as he saw the glimmer of tears floating in the depth of blue. *And this is the story that plays in my head every time I see that look in your eyes and want to wrap my arms around you. Because I like you more than I should. I'm feeling far more drawn to you than I've ever been to another human being. And I can't let an emotional connection to anyone cloud my professional judgment. I can't even let myself admit any of that out loud to you.*

"I'm sorry." Meg's voice was as soft as a whisper. Her words tickled at the base of his spine. Then she stood, slowly, and he felt the space between them shrink as she stepped into his chest. Every muscle in his body ached for the comfort of feeling her curled inside his arms.

Which made telling her what he needed to tell her next so much harder.

He took a step back. His hands clenched into fists. "Yeah. Me too. It's not a story I like telling, as you can imagine. But after everything the media put you and your family through, I wanted you to know." His knuckles cracked. "Anyway, there's something more I need to tell you, about the Raincoat Killer story specifically, and my reporting on it. When I told you that the Toronto police weren't thrilled with my story, I didn't fill you in about just how far and deep that resentment went, or what it means for me now. But first, I should probably go find some food. I haven't eaten since breakfast. What's next on your schedule?"

"There's a quick wedding rehearsal for Rachel and Wesley, followed by a small buffet-style rehearsal dinner. It should be done by nine o'clock and I have nothing on after that. But I should head over there in about fifteen minutes to make sure everything's going smoothly."

Hardly enough time to tell her everything he wanted her to know, but enough for a start.

"Okay. How about I go grab my stuff and then I'll walk you over? I'll give you the nutshell version on the way. Then maybe we can meet up afterward." *If you're still willing to talk to me.*

She nodded. "Okay. I'm going to go check out life jackets. See you in a second."

Then she disappeared behind a rack of paddles, before he thought to ask where the life jackets were. Oh well, if he got lost she was bound to come find him. He headed back through the store toward the office. Motion-sensor lights flickered on and off behind him. The tastefully cluttered store gave the customer the overall impression of having just wandered into a woodland outpost.

Walk five steps away from the big front windows, and you might as well be actually lost in the woods. He turned down an aisle, expecting to see the office door, and instead almost walked into a wall of fishing gear. He turned down another aisle and practically yelped in shock.

A figure stood in the shadows at the end of the aisle, next to the open office door, shrouded in a black rain slicker. Jack chuckled as he shook off the rush of adrenaline. He hadn't noticed a mannequin there earlier. Ironically, he'd probably been working feet away from it all afternoon and not even noticed. The hood was crooked. He reached up to straighten it.

A gloved hand grabbed Jack's wrist, and clamped down hard. The hood fell back, revealing a man in a black ski mask underneath. For a second Jack froze, and then he felt blood pounding hot and fierce in his heart. Jack wrenched his hand back, clenching his first and threw a punch into the man's masked face. "Meg! Run!"

But the words had barely left his mouth when he saw the flash of metal in the killer's hand and felt the sharp sting of a knife blade slice into his skin.

THIRTEEN

Jack's shout echoed through the store. Meg froze. She clamped her hand over her mouth to keep herself from shouting back and pressed herself back into the rack of life jackets. Her ears strained for his voice.

A grunt. A cry of pain. The sound of a shelf tipping over.

Where were they? Could she make it through the store to the front door without getting killed? And if she ran, what would happen to Jack? *Help us, Lord. Help Jack. Help me know what to do.* She slid her phone from her pocket and dialed nine-one-one, wincing as the sound of it ringing filled the air.

"Nine-one-one Emergency."

"This is Meg Duff," she hissed. "I'm in Extreme Sports Plus on Main Street. Someone's broken into the store." She closed her eyes. "Jack Brooks is here with me, and I think he's been attacked. Send the police. And an ambulance. It's life or death."

"Can you describe what's happening?"

No. She couldn't see. That was the problem. That and as long as she was holding the phone to her ear she couldn't possibly defend herself against whatever was out there, or help Jack. "Hurry!"

She hung up, then crawled through a wall of life jackets until she reached the end of the rack. She took a deep breath and climbed up to the top of a shelf of camping gear.

Her eyes searched the aisles. Then she saw them. The Raincoat Killer and Jack were locked in a desperate struggle for control. Jack was the stronger fighter. But it was clear he was on the defense, dodging and swerving to avoid the cruel, jagged edge of the killer's hunting knife. Fishing lures and netting spilled around them, nothing Jack could use as a weapon. Not against a knife anyway. But maybe she could help even the fight.

She braced her feet on the top of the shelf and gripped a low-hanging ceiling beam with one hand for balance. Then she grabbed a heavy kerosene lamp off the shelf, swung it around like a shot put and let it fly. It crashed into the rack behind them.

The Raincoat Killer's head snapped up toward her. Through the ski mask she could see his pierced lips part in a snarl. *Good luck climbing up here to get at me.* She paused in her tracks just long enough to watch as Jack sent a crushing blow into the back of the figure's head. Blood dripped from the killer's mouth. But the knife still hadn't left his grasp.

The killer swore loudly. He swung toward Jack. His blade flashed through the air.

She knew that voice. Why did she know that voice?

No time to think. She ran down to the end of the shelf, leaping over equipment and ducking under ceiling beams. A canoe and paddles hung in the air above her, suspended on interlocking chains. Guess she just had to hope Benji had used a solid anchor. She grabbed the side of the canoe and leapt, slithering into it on her stomach. The canoe swung wildly beneath her. She gritted her teeth and yanked a paddle from its mooring. "Jack! Up here!"

His eyes met hers. Strong. Unflinching. He pelted down the aisle toward her. The killer pounded after him. She let the paddle fly. The chains around her creaked. Jack caught the paddle by the shaft. The killer's knife flashed through the air, its blade aimed right between Jack's shoulder blades. But planting his feet, Jack spun backward, paddle gripped in both hands like a baseball bat. He swung and caught his assailant in the jaw. Jack's attacker dropped to the floor. The knife flew from his hand and skittered under the shelves.

The chains holding the canoe to the ceiling gave way. A desperate prayer slipped from Meg's lips.

The canoe fell. It crashed nose-first into the floor, tossing her out like a rag doll. Jarring pain filled her body.

For an agonizing moment, she lay there, unable to will her aching body to move. The back door slammed.

A strong hand brushed against her cheek "Meg?" She opened her eyes. Jack was kneeling on the floor beside her. "Are you all right? Can you move?"

She nodded. "Yeah, I think so. Just sore." She slowly pulled herself up to sitting. "Are you okay?"

"Yeah. Just a couple cuts and bruises."

"And the killer?"

"He got away. But he left the knife behind."

Meg let out a sigh of relief as she realized Benji's surveillance cameras would have caught the whole thing. She pressed her palms into the floor and tried to stand, but her shaking limbs refused to cooperate. She tried again, only to feel tears stream treacherously down her face.

"Hey, it's okay. Just give your body a minute." He brushed the tears from her cheeks, then pulled her into his arms. "I'm just thankful you're okay. That was the gutsiest thing I've ever seen."

"You needed some help to defend yourself. It was the fastest way. I figured, if need be, I could stay up there and hide until the police arrived to rescue me." She let her body curl against him. She could feel his heartbeat racing through his chest. "Would have been even better if the canoe hadn't fallen off the ceiling."

He chuckled. His lips brushed across the top of her head. "You are one of the bravest people I've ever met. You might have saved my life, you know." His face was so close she could feel his breath her neck.

She shivered. "You seemed to be doing just fine."

"It was like knowing you were somewhere in the store, in danger too, made me fight harder than I've fought against anything in my life." He brushed his lips along her hairline. "It made me feel stronger. Like I could take on an army of killers single-handedly if that's what it took to keep you safe."

Blood was seeping through his sleeve. A sob rose in her chest. If he hadn't been thinking of her, would he have managed to escape without getting hurt? Ever since she'd met him he'd been in danger, and it was always because he was trying to protect her. How many times would he keep on throwing himself into harm's way for her before it finally caught up with him?

Sirens wailed in the distance. She pushed him back. "Thank you for protecting me. But I need you to stop. Okay? Please. Don't keep risking your life because of me." She forced her body to stand. "You're not the police, Jack. You're not my brother. Let alone my personal bodyguard. I think you should go back to Toronto. I think you should drop this story and forget you ever met me. For your own sake."

Red-and-blue lights filled the window, sending waves of light over the confused, hurt depths of Jack's eyes. Her knees buckled, and for a moment she thought she was about to tumble back into his arms. Instead she turned and ran to open the door for the officers.

FOURTEEN

A deep purple filled the clouds above her head. The fiery red sun disappeared into the lake below her feet. Meg stood alone on the second floor of the pavilion's wrought-iron staircase. Beside her, sweeping doors led through to the second-story reception hall. Rachel and Wesley's rehearsal dinner was in full swing. Meg, their wedding planner, was missing it.

The wedding party had already been at the church with the pastor by the time she'd reached Benji on his cell phone. Her brother told her they'd gone ahead and started the rehearsal without her. There didn't seem to be any point in interrupting them. When Officer Burne had arrived on the scene at the shop, he'd offered to call his daughter-in-law, Alyssa, the aspiring wedding planner, and ask her to go ahead to the pavilion and make sure everything was ready for the party. Meg had felt too numb to disagree.

Should a young couple be forced to delay their

wedding rehearsal because of something their wedding planner had been caught up in? Should it impact their wedding? What if someone else was able to step in and keep things running smoothly? The more she turned the question around in her mind, the worse it sounded.

It had taken the paramedics almost half an hour to conclude she had nothing more serious than a few scrapes and bruises. Then the police had questioned her for over an hour. Once again, they'd separated her from Jack, almost from the moment they arrived, and this time she'd been questioned by a nonislander, Detective Owen Ravine, who'd apparently been brought in from Toronto to help with the investigation. The experience was a whole lot different than being questioned by men she'd known all her life. He'd had a lot of questions about Jack and just how well she really knew him.

Shivers ran up her arms. She pulled her shawl tighter around her shoulders. When she'd dashed home to get changed, the emerald-green party dress and ivory wrap had seemed perfect for the muggy evening. Now it was all she could do to keep her arms from shaking. It had been like this when Benji was in the hospital. She'd always been cold, even in the heat of summer, with a chill in her arms that had never really left her.

"Waiting for someone?" A warm voice floated up the staircase toward her. She looked down. Jack was coming up the stairs two at a time. He'd also changed and was now in simple tan slacks and a blue button-down. "How are you?"

"I'm fine." She forced a smile. "Clean bill of health. Benji got the surveillance tapes to the police. Insurance will cover any damage to the store. Everything's just fine. Benji also swears the entire wedding party was with him on the boat this afternoon, so there's no way either Duncan or Wesley could be the man who attacked you." She frowned. "Unfortunately I'm also now two hours late for this wedding rehearsal. I'll be lucky if Rachel doesn't fire me." She turned toward the door. But as she reached for the handle, she felt his hand touch her wrist.

"Are you sure you're okay?"

She shrugged her shoulders lightly, but he didn't let go. "Of course. I'm fine."

Jack took another step toward her. "No, you're not. You shouldn't feel you need to pretend you are either." His fingers slid slowly up her arm, the simple gesture filling her with warmth. "No one would be fine after what you've been through." His hand came to rest on her shoulder. "It's okay to admit that."

She pressed her lips together as sudden tears rushed to her eyes. She blinked them back. If she started crying now, she'd never stop. "I'm not going to fall apart."

"No one's asking you to. But you've been through more in a couple of days than most people go through in a lifetime. Most people wouldn't even be standing, let alone still trying to keep someone else's wedding going." His fingers tenderly brushed along her shoulder blade, melting the tension from her limbs. "It's okay to hit Pause for a moment and give yourself permission to be human."

She closed her eyes, took a deep breath and held it for a moment. *It is well, it is well, with my soul....* She exhaled slowly. His gaze was still focused on her face with an affection and intensity that made her feel so safe and yet so afraid that if she wasn't careful she'd just fall into his arms. It would be so easy to let her guard down, lean her body into his chest and let him be strong enough for the both of them.

But he wasn't her rock, her fortress or her anchor. He was just some daredevil reporter who was here today, and off chasing another life-threatening story tomorrow. She rolled her shoulders back. "There will be plenty of time to be human after this wedding is over."

She opened the door and walked into the rehearsal-dinner party. A few dozen people were milling around the beautiful wooden room, listening to the gentle strains of a jazz quartet and helping themselves to pastries from the dessert carts.

Most of the guests were older islanders, friends of Rachel's grandmother and members of prominent island families. She wondered how many would be gossiping about the death of old man McCarthy.

The wedding party were off in a world of their own, the group of young people seemingly determined to avoid contact with anyone older than twenty-two. Duncan's eyes were locked on his smartphone. Fiona was standing at the window, staring out at the beach, idly picking food off her plate. Rachel clutched her groom's arm, a barely concealed sulk on her pretty pink lips. Meg found herself wondering, yet again, what kind of wedding Rachel and Wesley would have chosen for themselves if the lure of her family's money hadn't brought them to the island.

"Oh, Meg!" Rachel's voice echoed through the room, in a high-pitched shriek halfway between a cry and a shout. "You poor thing!" She waved a hand at the quartet. The music stopped cold. The young bride rushed toward her while the whole room seemed to turn en mass and stare at her. A flush rose to Meg's cheeks. Rachel threw her arms around her and squeezed her so tightly it almost pinched. "When Alyssa told me about the break-in at the store, I couldn't believe it! You would think a place like that would have better security!" Meg tried to slide out of her grasp. Rachel only let her go partway, gripping her shoulders, holding her at arm's length. "I just hope none of this has any impact on the wedding tomorrow. It won't, right?"

Was she that selfish and shallow or just very, very young?

Then Meg realized how pale Rachel's face was beneath the immaculate makeup and that her hands were so tense they were almost shaking. Wesley was still standing, paralyzed, where his fiancée had left him. Rachel must be worried sick. Her groom seemed lost and confused. Guilt stabbed Meg's heart. This was a woman whose mother had died and whose father had abandoned her. She'd probably been waiting her whole life for her wedding day, only to find it threatened by things beyond her control. "I'm sure everything will be fine."

"Of course it will be," a commanding voice sounded in her ear. She turned. Malcolm Burne was standing by her shoulder, with a stunning, tall redhead. "Meg, I'd like you to meet my wife, Alyssa."

"Nice to meet you," Alyssa practically gushed. Perfectly manicured hands grabbed Meg's and held them. Officer Burne's daughter-in-law was several years younger than Meg, with high cheekbones and a wide mouth. "I'm happy to help with anything you need. I've already told Rachel and Wesley I can step in and take over arrangements for tomorrow. From the looks of things here tonight, you've done such a good job of organizing everything, Meg, the wedding could practically run itself."

Meg planted her heels into the hardwood. A sick, unsettling feeling was crawling up the base of her spine.

"In fact—" Malcolm's hand fell on her shoulder "—as we told my father, Alyssa is happy to take on any other weddings you have coming up until you're fully back on your feet again. As a cop myself, I assure you there's nothing worse than feeling like you're rushed into getting over trauma."

"Trauma!" Rachel practically shrieked. "What trauma? What happened? I thought it was just a break-in." The scream seemed to unstick Wesley, who rushed across the room to join them, Fiona and Duncan on his heels.

Meg turned toward her. "It's nothing too serious. The paramedics checked me out, and I'm fine."

Alyssa's unnaturally green eyes grew wide. Her husband, Malcolm, lifted one immaculate eyebrow. The couple shared a meaningful glance. Okay, so presumably they knew about what had happened at McCarthy's last night, the attack on the ferry and what had just happened in the store. Was that all they knew?

"Are you sure?" Rachel's eyes suddenly latched on to Meg's face, focusing on her with such intensity that Meg instinctively wanted to look away. "Is there something you're not telling me? Is everything okay?"

No. Everything is definitely not okay. I'm scared. I'm tired. Scratch that, I'm exhausted. All I want to do right now is curl up and cry. I've been terrified and terrorized by a killer in a raincoat. And I really don't want to be your wedding planner.

She shot a glance over to where Jack still stood in the partially open doorway. He stepped through, letting the door swing shut behind him. A question echoed in his eyes. She looked away.

A tight smile spread across her lips. "Don't worry about me. I'll do whatever it takes to make sure your wedding is perfect."

Rachel grinned.

Fiona screamed. Suddenly. Terribly. Her dinner plate smashed to the floor. Her hand shook as she pointed to where Jack stood, his back to the door.

A figure in a raincoat was standing at the door behind him.

Jack turned. Disbelief filled his gut, even as his mind registered the tall, raincoat-clad figure standing just inches away, on the other side of a thin sheet of window glass. Despite Fiona's scream of shock, she, Meg and the party guests were far enough away from the window that all they could probably see was a silhouette. But for Jack, it was all too clear. The same raincoat. The same black face mask. The bloody, pierced lip still visibly sore, damaged from the punch Jack had leveled earlier when he was fighting for his life. Bloodshot eyes so wide from drug abuse and rage their irises were all but gone.

After all the care he'd shown getting his victims alone, surely the Raincoat Killer was too smart for a public stunt like this. Was he too angry to think straight? Too high on drugs and alcohol to even know what he was doing? So evil he no longer cared about being seen?

Jack set his jaw. His hand clenched into fists. The killer's eyes narrowed.

Whatever his reason, he wasn't going to get away this time.

Jack yanked the door open. The killer turned and ran.

Jack chased after him, pelting down the wrought-iron stairs. He could hear voices yelling behind him. Malcolm Burne shouted at him to stop.

He didn't stop. He didn't even turn.

He was a good twenty pounds of muscle larger than the young cop and he had a head start. He was only half a flight of steps behind the killer. Either he stopped the maniac or no one would. Jack threw himself down the stairs, barely feeling the steps under his feet.

The Raincoat Killer hit the boardwalk and stumbled to his knees. He tumbled off the deck, dragged himself up out of the sand and tore across the beach like a terrified rodent.

Jack's feet hit the boards. He leapt, landed hard on the Raincoat Killer's back and brought him to the ground. The killer swung backward and caught Jack in the chin. Pain shot through the reporter's jaw. But Jack gritted his teeth. He slammed the killer's face into the sand. Rolled him over. Yanked off his hood.

And stared into the ugly, bloody face of local teenager Kenny Smythe.

Did this mean the Raincoat Killer was nothing but a petty teenaged drug dealer from Manitoulin Island? Or that a local teenaged criminal just happened to dress up in a raincoat, sneak into Benji's store and threaten Jack with a knife?

"None of this makes any sense." Jack shook his head at the thin, dark-haired Toronto detective named Owen Ravine, now sitting across the table from him, hoping the so-called crime expert would be able to shed some light on the increasingly murky situation. Detective Ravine frowned. Jack dropped his head into his hands and stared down at the table in front of him.

When he'd seen the drug-addled teenager, down in the sand, begging for mercy, it had taken all the self-control Jack possessed not to punch him. Instead he'd restrained both Kenny and himself, until young Officer Burne had stepped in and taken over. It was only then that he'd seen the wall of faces watching from the second-story balcony. Meg was staring down at him. Her hands clutched the railing. The look on her face inscrutable. Then she'd disappeared into the crowd.

Officers Stephen and Malcolm Burne forced Kenny into the back of a cop car. Detective Ravine kindly requested Jack join him for a chat in an empty room on the pavilion's main floor.

The wiry Toronto detective had very long fingers and jet-black hair that grayed slightly at the temples. Jack had heard of him but wasn't sure he'd ever met him. While Ravine did look vaguely familiar, the reporter had seen enough senior detectives at enough crime scenes that after a while they all kind of blended into one. While they tended to know more about investigations than your average cop, they were also a lot harder to get information from, making them less useful as potential sources. Jack preferred beat cops— they saw a lot, and were more willing to talk. He couldn't remember the last time he was actually alone with a detective.

Hopefully this one would actually be willing to listen.

"At the moment, Mr. Brooks, the young man is claiming he was framed."

Jack's head jerked up. "He what?"

Detective Ravine shrugged. "Kenny Smythe claims that someone approached him a few hours ago, asking to score some drugs. Things get a bit sketchy after that, because apparently Kenny took a lot of those drugs himself. But apparently this person also offered him a couple hundred dollars to dress up in a raincoat, sneak into the sports store, find Meg Duff and scare the life out of her."

"He confessed to attacking me at the sports store?"

"Yup. But he says you laid hands on him first, and he was only acting in self-defense."

"He had a knife!" Jack leapt out of his seat.

The detective waved him down. "Relax. I've reviewed the surveillance tape. It's pretty clear what went down. He's lucky he made it out with just a bloody lip."

Jack landed hard on the plastic chair. "What was he doing at the pavilion?"

"Again, his train of thought is a bit hard to follow, probably from the mountains of cocaine he appears to have taken to dull the pain after your fight. It appears he became enraged his contact didn't get in touch to pay up and went storming around the island in a stupor trying to find him, which is how he ended up at the pavilion. Where you—" he looked down at his notes "—and I quote, 'viciously jumped him like a crazy person.'" He smiled a thin-lipped smile.

Jack didn't smile back. "At least tell me you know who hired him."

"He claims it was 'Jack Brooklyn, the reporter from Toronto.'"

"You're kidding." Jack glanced at the ceiling and muttered a prayer for patience. "The thug didn't even get my name right."

The detective couldn't possibly believe Kenny was telling the truth. Why was someone coming after him? Why try to discredit him this way? Jack closed his eyes. *Lord, You are the one who can see order in the chaos. There has to be a pattern here. There has to be a truth hidden in this darkness. Help me find the truth that I need to see.*

"Unfortunately for him," Ravine said, "a man named Benji Duff swears you can't have been wandering around the island hiring drug addicts today, because you spent all afternoon researching leads in his office."

Jack opened his eyes. A picture began to form in his mind's eye, as if he were peering down through the water in the lake, at the stones that now lay at his feet.

What if his research had actually uncovered something, and he just hadn't realized it? What if he'd stumbled onto something important, gotten too close to the truth and had accidentally tipped off the real Raincoat Killer? What if the killer had then retaliated by hiring a local drug dealer and thug to go after Meg?

The picture in his mind grew murky again. Even if his theory was correct, it still didn't explain why.

"Please tell me you're taking this seriously. Tell me you're going to find out who hired Kenny, and what link that person might have to the Raincoat Killer murders."

"Trust me, Mr. Brooks, we're taking this very seriously." The detective leaned back. "We will find out who hired him. He's called in a lawyer, so it may take a few days and some deal making. But we'll find out eventually. Unfortunately for Kenny Smythe, he just turned eighteen a few weeks ago, so we pressed the fact that he was facing an adult sentence pretty hard. Hopefully that'll get through to him." He slid his business card across the table. "In the meantime, this is my personal cell phone number. I'll be assisting local officers up here for as long as it takes to sort this entire mess out thoroughly. Feel free to call me directly if you come up with any new leads you think I should be chasing. You've opened a whole new can of worms for us in the last few days, and the chief back in Toronto has put me in charge of sorting them out." His chair scraped back. "But we'll get it sorted, and the truth will come out in the end. Don't worry. We'll find out who hired this kid. We'll find out if any of this is related to the murders in Toronto, or the other incidents on the island. Just be patient and let justice take its course. It all might just take some time."

Time. That was the one thing Jack was sure he didn't have.

FIFTEEN

The pavilion's second-story restaurant was deserted. Meg had sent the catering crew home early and the cleaners weren't expected for almost another hour. The main lights were off, but small bulbs still glowed over the buffet table. Half-empty plates lay on tables. Two full dessert trolleys still stood by the wall. She walked over, picked up a plate and took a forkful of cake. It was delicious.

Footsteps behind her. She turned. Jack was standing in the doorway.

"You want chocolate cake, lemon slice or pear tart?"

"Excuse me?"

She pushed one of each onto a plate, then walked over and handed it to him. "The caterer gets paid whether we eat it or not. I just have to hope that Rachel's grandmother doesn't refuse to pay. Otherwise I'll have to cover it out of pocket or risk getting sued by the caterer."

"I suppose they could sue Kenny Smythe and me instead."

"Don't even joke."

He took a bite of tart, chewed it thoughtfully and then swallowed. "This is good. Really good. Come to think of it, I don't think I've eaten since breakfast." For that matter, neither had she. "So, how up to speed are you on what's been happening?"

"You mean the Raincoat Killer?" she asked. She turned her fork slowly on her plate. "I know Kenny Smythe confessed to attacking you in the store and that he's been arrested. He'll probably be stuck sitting in that cell for a long time too. Local police have probably been just itching for him to turn eighteen." She sighed. "I also know the police still have no clue who attacked me on the ferry, as it probably wasn't Kenny. I know they're still not ready to believe us when we say that McCarthy's death might not have been a suicide. I also briefly met that detective that came up from Toronto, Owen Ravine?" She shrugged. "I don't quite know how to put this, but I've stopped feeling like any of the police up here are really listening to me. It's like they've all gone from people I've known my whole life to virtual strangers."

"That's probably because of me." He finished the tart, then tried the cake. "Like I mentioned before, I have to fill you in on something that's happening in Toronto, in relation to my job, how the police there reacted to my initial story, and the fallout ever since." He groaned. "I don't even know where to start. I've been questioned by police so many times in the past forty-eight hours I can hardly string my thoughts together, let alone try to put them in a coherent sentence."

"I know how you feel. Can it wait until after the wedding tomorrow? Or at least until we've both had a good night's sleep? At least until my head stops buzzing? Right now everything feels like white noise." She set down her plate. "Come on. Let me show you something."

She crossed the room to a small door in the wall, felt for a light switch and then led him up a narrow spiral staircase to the small observatory deck on the pavilion's top floor. She switched off the light again. The island spread out beneath them in all directions. To their left, the gentle lights of town faded out into the woods beyond. On the right, the bay spread out below them like a roll of blue-black velvet. A scattering of boats floated over the surface like candles.

She leaned on the window ledge and stared out into the night. "Welcome to my favorite hiding spot. I've always loved coming up here, looking out at the beach, watching people out on the water…" Her voice caught in her throat. "When I was a teenager, I used to really love watching extreme water sports—before Benji's accident. But I knew if my mom caught me down on the beach, she'd stand there and lecture me loudly about how dangerous and reckless they were. So I used to sneak up here just to get a bird's-eye view of the daredevils zipping along on personal watercraft and water skis, or flying past me on parasails." She frowned. "Hard to believe now, isn't it?"

She could feel Jack step toward her. The space between them shrank. The heat of him seemed to radiate through her back. Comforting. Strengthening.

"It wasn't that my mom actually didn't want me parasailing or waterskiing or anything like that. 'Not until you're older.' She didn't outright forbid me. But I knew if I did it would upset her. So I didn't try. My mother carries this sense of fear around with her everywhere she goes, like an invisible scarf wrapped around her neck.

"I promised myself I'd never be like her. When Benji, my little brother, bucked Mom's disapproval and just went ahead and tackled every extreme sport that he could, even though he was only a kid, I was so proud of him." Her shoulders shook as she could feel the threat of tears building in her eyes. She blinked hard but not before one managed to slip down her cheek. "Now my little brother has turned out to be exactly the man he always said he'd become. And I'm the woman I promised myself I'd never be."

His hand brushed her shoulder, turning her toward him. The darkness of the skies outside reflected in his eyes. "Come here." His voice was husky. "You could probably use a hug. I know I could." He spread his arms to make room for her. She stepped inside them, letting her head fall against the strength of his chest.

What was it about having his arms around her that made her feel so safe, so comforted...even made her feel small? Both her father and brother were big men. Yet, for as long as she could remember, she'd felt the need to care for them, to be the glue that held everything in place and the cornerstone that kept the house from falling.

Her mother had hovered around her father like a hummingbird. Fretting over how the dinner was cooked or the house was cleaned. Never pausing long enough for something as simple as a hug. Then, with Benji's accident, her mother had fallen apart. So Meg had stepped up. Made the meals. Done the shopping. Opened the mail, placing the bills in a tidy pile on her father's desk. Hid the newspapers when they arrived. While her brother's physical strength and bulk might have eclipsed her physically by the time they were teenagers, he was still her little brother. He brought out her protective instincts. She even did his laundry.

But Jack was a man. All man. In a way she couldn't put a finger on, and didn't know how to explain in words. His unshaven cheek brushed against the top of her head, ruffling her hair. His lips hovered over her forehead, tenderly, affectionately. What was she thinking bringing a man like him, alone, into her private, dark sanctuary? Jack was the kind of man who acted impulsively, instinctively. Who'd catapulted off the ferry to save her. Who'd chased Kenny down the beach without a second's thought. But she wasn't like that, was she? No, she planned ahead. She thought things through. She never let herself get caught off guard.

So what was she doing here, with him, alone? And why couldn't she muster the resolve to pull away?

Her eyes closed. His hand slid along her neck, burying his fingers into her hair, twisting gently through the tendrils at the back of her neck. An unfamiliar ache tugged inside her chest. What would it be like not to be in control? To let go of the reins?

She tilted her face toward him. He kissed her. Sweetly. Gently. Asking nothing from her in return but the willingness to let herself be held. A deep sigh spread through her body. Her body melted into his. Her limbs let go of the tension that had held her in its grip for so long.

She wanted this. She'd always wanted this. To be able to let go and let someone else catch her, support her, hold her, even for a moment, knowing he wouldn't push her or take from her, leaving her depleted and empty.

But could she really entrust him with that? Yes, he'd saved her life. She owed him that much.

But how was kissing her now any less impulsive or reckless than chasing after a serial killer or jumping overboard? Jack was impulsive. He'd kissed her impulsively. Nothing more.

Hot tears pushed their way to her lids. She pushed him back. "I'm sorry…" she gasped. "I can't. I just can't."

He stepped back. His face paled as if she'd verbally slapped him. "You can't what?"

Couldn't let herself be with him and couldn't stop herself from falling for him.

"I can't have a relationship with a man who just goes through life thoughtlessly, and recklessly throws himself into danger. Who goes bungee-jumping off cliffs and chases killers down the beach. Not after what happened to my brother."

His expression hardened. "And what happened to your brother, Meg? Last time I checked, Benji was just fine. Yes, he was hurt fourteen years ago. Terribly hurt. I'm not about to trivialize what happened to him or what you all went through. But he *healed,* Meg. He grew up. He went on and built an amazing life for himself. While it's like you're still there, standing in the snow, staring at the crash, waiting for someone to give you permission to get on with your life."

Tears cascaded down her cheeks. She didn't even try to wipe them back. "That's not fair."

"Isn't it? Are you telling me you wouldn't react differently right now if I promised to give up sports, all sports, for you? What if I promised to give up being a crime reporter too? What if I promised I would just sit quietly and safely behind my desk and never take another risk for the rest of my long, boring life, just because you asked me to?"

Her eyes shot up to his face, unexpected hope leaping in her chest. "Would you?"

"No. And that's my point."

A gasp slipped through her lips. "How dare you?"

"I'm sorry." His voice softened. "Look, Meg, yes, I have been living like a bachelor. I own a motorcycle, not a car. I take on the toughest possible assignments. I venture into war zones and gang territories. I go there because other people can't, and the stories need to be told. All too often other reporters can't hack it or they have families to come home to, and I don't. I'm not in a position to consider making a commitment to anyone right now. My job at the newspaper is way too shaky—

thanks to the Raincoat Killer story. And yes, I'm every bit as into extreme sports as your brother and every bit as serious about safety gear, as well." His fingers brushed away tears from the corner of her eyes. "But when I'm in a secure enough place that I can ask someone to be my partner, my wife, some of that would change. I would have to consider her and our children in every risk I took and every decision I made. She would be my priority.

"But with me as her husband, Meg. Her partner. Someone worthy of her trust and her respect. Not as some fragile thing she thinks she has to hover over and fret over, like your mother hovered over your father, or how you hover over your brother. Not with a woman who's going to question and second-guess every single choice I made. Your brother may be willing to accept you mothering him. I wouldn't. No man who's worthy of winning your heart ever will. And until you move past your fears, you'll never be ready to find the kind of happiness and life you deserve."

A flame of heat rose to her cheeks.

Loud banging sounded from downstairs. Someone was knocking on the door leading to the second floor of the pavilion. *The cleaners!* She heard a voice calling her name. She pulled away from Jack and ran for the stairs. The sound grew louder. The door must have locked behind Jack when he'd

come through. She ran down the stairs, even as
Jack called for her to wait. She tumbled back into
the second-story dining room and was partway
across the floor when she realized it wasn't the
cleaners at the door, but Stuart Smythe.

Kenny's younger brother stood there, shivering
in a sleeveless white T-shirt. The fifteen-year-old's
face was a sickly shade of yellow in the glare of
the pavilion's fluorescent lights.

"Meg! What did you do to my brother? Why
is he in jail?" Stuart was drunk, probably high,
definitely scared, and trying to hide it all under a
whole lot of bravado. Poor kid. He was used to following around in Kenny's shadow, and the news
that the police were actually keeping him in jail
and threatening him with adult charges was probably a major shock to the teenager's system.

Her feet slowed. "I didn't do anything to your
brother, Stuart. He's been arrested. But I'm sure
the police are going to take good care of him. Nobody's going to hurt him. He just needs to be honest with them and everything will be okay."

Stuart grumbled something under his breath.
He stepped back from the door. His shoulders fell.

Jack's hand brushed her elbow. "Should we call
the police?"

She watched as Stuart walked down the platform
a few steps, then turned around and walked back.

"Look at him," she said. "He's just a scared kid. He's not carrying a weapon and I'm not about to open the door."

Besides, Jack could probably take him with a single blow if he needed to.

"Stuart." She stepped up to the window. "It's going to be okay. I promise."

"They wouldn't let me see him." He sniffed. "Or my dad. Or mom. Just some lawyer."

Wow. So they really were clamping down hard. "I'm sorry. That must be hard. I'm sure they'll let him see your parents tomorrow."

"My dad says that the lawyer said you accused Kenny of helping a serial killer!" His voice rose. "A serial killer! One who attacked you and killed old man McCarthy and a bunch of women! My brother wouldn't do that! He wouldn't help no serial killer!" He hit the glass with both hands. It shook under his weight. "He said they could lock him up for a long time! Like the rest of his life. For being an accessory. My brother's no accessory to nothing!"

No wonder the teenager was terrified. The police had played hardball with his brother, the news of which had then gotten filtered through a lawyer, his father and finally into a fifteen-year-old bundle of aggression who'd fueled himself up with drugs and alcohol.

She tried to take another step toward the glass, only to find herself stopped by Jack's grip on her elbow. "Okay," she said. "I understand why you're scared. But all your brother has to do is tell the police the truth and he'll probably end up with nothing more than a drug charge."

Which probably wouldn't do Kenny any harm.

"Did you do it?" Stuart was practically screaming now. "Did you tell the police that there was a serial killer on the island? And that you knew all about it?"

"Sort of. But it's not like—"

"Why would you do that?" His voice bellowed through the night air and over the empty beach. "Why would you lie? Why would you hurt my brother like that?"

Her eyes glanced back to Jack's face. It was grim. As much as she didn't want to add to this kid's problems by calling the police on him, if he didn't calm down they'd have no choice.

"Do you know who hired your brother?" Jack's voice was steady. "If you did, and you tell the police, they might let your brother go."

The teenager's head shook as if there were water in his ears. "Maybe. I don't know. He told me not to tell anyone anything. To just say it was some reporter guy."

Jack took a deep breath. "Listen, I'm the reporter your brother fought with." Jack walked toward the door with a calm authority that sent shivers down her spine. "I'm not out to hurt you or Kenny. I promise. If you tell the police everything you know, I give you my word that I'll tell the police I'm dropping the charges against him for attacking me."

Stuart's eyes narrowed. "I'm not gonna talk to the police."

"Then talk to me." Jack raised both hands in front of him, palms up. "You tell me what you know and I'll tell the police for you."

"And you'll tell the police to let him out of jail for cutting you?"

"I can't control what the police are going to do. But I promise to talk to them about dropping the assault charges, yes."

Stuart's lip jutted out. She could see his tongue rolling over his teeth as though he was debating whether to swallow what he was hearing. "What about wrecking the store?"

Meg took a deep breath. "I'll talk to my brother. You know Benji, Stuart. He's a good guy. He believes God gives everyone second chances."

"And my brother won't be mad?"

"I don't know," Meg said softly. "But trust me, please. I promise you, telling the truth is the best thing for everyone, including your brother."

Stuart clenched his eyes shut. Meg held her breath.

"Okay. Fine." Stuart nodded. "I'll do it."

"Thank You, God." Jack reached for the door handle.

A gunshot cracked the silent air. Stuart's body wheeled suddenly. The teenager screamed. A second shot. Stuart fell backward over the balcony. Jack's arms flew around Meg, pulling her down.

Glass exploded around them.

SIXTEEN

She was cold on the inside, with the same numbing chill that had first slipped inside her limbs when she paced the hospital floor waiting for news of her brother. Her limbs felt frozen to her side. Her mind was a pool of black, floating with disjointed images and sensations.

Stuart screaming. Glass falling. Jack pulling her to him, tightly, telling her it was going to be okay. The sound of sirens. Flashing lights. Stuart's body on a stretcher. A blanket being draped around her shoulders. Jack refusing to let her go. Sitting in the back of a vehicle. Her brother's voice. A pillow underneath her head. Something warm and comforting over her. Then the gentle sound of flames crackling.

She opened her eyes and waited as the images around her began to come into focus. She was lying on the couch in her own living room. Harry was curled up beside her. The dog's head was on her legs. His soulful eyes watched her face. Jack was crouched by the fireplace, nursing a fire to life.

"Stuart!"

In an instant, Jack had crossed the floor and was kneeling by her side. "Meg, it's okay. The paramedics got to him really fast. He's in the hospital."

"Is he alive?"

"Last I heard, unconscious but still alive." Jack's hand brushed her cheek. "How are you?"

"Okay." She stretched her limbs, linking her fingers together and extending her arms down toward her toes. Harry tumbled off her and onto the floor. "I thought I heard Benji?"

"You did. I called him right after I hung up with nine-one-one. The paramedics wanted to take you to the hospital, but he helped me convince them you'd feel better sooner if we brought you home."

At least she could be grateful for that. She pressed the tips of her fingers together, then rolled her shoulders back.

"Your brother went downstairs about half an hour ago." Jack sat down cross-legged on the floor beside her. "He sat on the couch with you for a while and talked to you while you dozed a bit. Then I told him to go sleep and that I'd stay up with you for a bit. It's after midnight."

"I don't really remember all of that. It's like I've been only half-awake."

"You were in shock, hon. That was pretty understandable and a very normal reaction. You saw someone you know nearly get killed. It was pretty horrendous, especially on top of everything that has already happened over the past few days."

"Someone shot Stuart." The words fell from her lips like iron.

"Yeah. Someone did. Two shots. The first caught him in the shoulder and knocked him off the balcony. Second took out a window." Jack's tone was soft, but his words were direct and un-flinching. "The shots came from below. Probably a handgun. The police think someone was hiding in the darkness and listening in on our conversation. Probably whoever hired his brother to pretend to be the Raincoat Killer. Whatever reason someone had to get Kenny to attack us and then implicate me, obviously they meant business."

Memories of the past few hours were filtering back into her brain now. Disjointed. Like snap-shots from a nightmare. She pulled her knees into her chest and rested her chin on top of them. One moment she'd been standing there, asking this teenager to open up to them and trust her. The next, he was shot. She stared into the fire. The fragments flying through her memory paused, on one crystal-clear sensation—Jack's fingers brush-ing through her hair as he held her to him tightly. He'd been there. With her. He'd held her tightly through the whole ordeal, without once letting her go. "You stayed with me, every single second."

"Of course I did."

"But you're a crime reporter and that was a crime scene!" Her words flew out in a rush. "You didn't have to stay with me. You could have tried taking statements. You could have followed the ambulance to the hospital. You could have gone to the police station to see what you were able to find out, or…"

His hands reached for hers, enveloping them. "But I didn't." Light and shadows danced along his jaw. "Because you needed me and that was more important."

"But this is all my fault." Her voice came out as a whisper.

"Honey, none of this is your fault."

"Yes, it is." She pulled her hands back and wrapped them around herself. "If I'd let you interview me about being attacked by the Raincoat Killer, on the night it happened, your paper would have run it immediately, right?"

He nodded slowly. "It would have been up on our website within the hour, yes."

"Then other press would have picked it up?"

"Most definitely."

"Then the entire island would have been gossiping about it by this morning, which means no one would have been able to bribe Kenny into dressing up in a raincoat like that. The Smythe brothers are criminal, but they're not stupid enough to intentionally get mixed up in something big like that. Especially not for a measly couple hundred dollars. Then Kenny wouldn't be in jail and Stuart would never have been shot." She hugged her knees to her chest. A tear rolled down her cheek. "They saw us after we swam to shore. They even asked me why I was muddy. If only I'd told them the truth…"

"Meg. Don't do this." His hand brushed against her arms.

"Interview me."

His spine straightened. "What?"

"I think you should interview me. Right now. I can't expect this story to stay secret forever. You said so yourself. This whole thing is spinning out of control. More people have gotten hurt, and the longer I try to keep what happened to me a secret, the greater the chance that someone else is going to die."

He knelt beside her, peeled her hands away from their desperate clutch on her legs and held them tightly in his, "Are you sure?"

Her lips quivered. "No, I'm not. I'm terrified."

"Why?"

"I'm not good at this." She shook her head. "At words. At telling people how I feel or explaining what happened. Don't you get that? You say that telling our stories can help free us and other people. I've now seen what happens when people try to keep quiet and hide things they shouldn't. But saying the wrong thing is equally dangerous. If you stick a microphone in my face, who knows what I'll say? I get muddled. I get flustered. I get my words wrong, and say the opposite of what I mean sometimes. What if I say the wrong thing? What if I make everything worse?"

"Meg? Do you trust me?" Dark eyes looked deeply into hers, tender, protective, filled with a depth of unspoken emotion that made her heart leap painfully inside her chest.

Did she trust him? This man who had not only risked his life to save her, but refused to let her go when chaos rained down around them.

She nodded. "I do. I trust you."

"Then trust me with this. You've got to know I'm nothing like the reporters that went tramping through your flower bed and trampling over your life, just to stick a microphone in your face and trick you into saying things you never meant to say. I would never do anything to hurt you." She tried to look down at her feet again, but he tilted her face up, until her eyes met his. "Trust me with your story. Let it all pour out like a giant mess of sand, and rocks, and clay. I will search through it for the gems. I will polish your words. I will shape them. Not just because it's my job, but because it's my privilege. To take your words and make them beautiful."

Sobs broke over Meg's body like a wave. The sadness and fear, which had hidden somewhere inside her for so very long, burst through her body, pushing her off the couch, onto the floor and into the safety of Jack's arms. "But it was my fault. It was always my fault."

His arms tightened around her. "What was?"

"Benji's accident. It's my fault he was out on Chris's snowmobile that day. My fault he got hurt. My fault Chris died." Fresh tears filled her eyes again. His fingers stroked through her hair, gently, firmly. She swallowed hard. "Remember how I told you I used to sneak up to the pavilion to watch the daredevils? Chris was my favorite. I had the biggest schoolgirl crush on him. He was gutsy, and a risk taker, and the absolute opposite of everything I'd been raised to be.

"He asked me out on a date. I was seventeen. I wanted to, but I had to say no. My parents wouldn't let me, because he had a reputation for being reckless and driving dangerously. He'd already been in two car accidents. They didn't want me to get hurt."

She sat back, just enough to look up into his eyes. His arms slid down her body. His hands rested gently against the small of her back.

"He kept asking me out. Over and over again.

Surprising me places. Following me. He was tenacious like that. He didn't give up when he wanted something, especially because he knew I liked him too. And I fell apart. Completely." She wiped the back of her hand over her eyes. "I didn't know what to do. So I told Benji. He was my little brother and my best friend. He found me crying in my room one day, and demanded that we talk about it. So I told him everything. Absolutely everything.

"He was only fifteen! But he seemed so grown-up, trying to take care of me and fix everything for me. He was already into extreme sports anyway. He figured if he got to know Chris better and if they became friends, then maybe he could convince Chris to back down a bit. And if he was in our house more as Benji's friend, then maybe my parents would see he wasn't such a bad guy, and then I could date him...." She sniffed. "He was doing it for me. But I was his big sister, Jack. I should never have told him all that. He was too young to know what to do about it. I should have been looking out for him. I should have protected him."

Jack's lips brushed over her forehead. "Oh, honey, you do try to take on responsibility for the whole world, don't you? You know it's not your fault. If Benji was just a kid at the time, then so were you. And even if Benji was trying to help by becoming friends with Chris, the responsibility was still on the two of them to be safe when they went off together. They are the ones who chose not to wear helmets and to ride off the trails. The truck driver is the one who didn't stop in time. All the fallout to your father's business and all the irresponsible press coverage was due to other people's choices."

"I missed Chris a lot after he died." She sniffed. "I felt guilty about it too. Because I liked him, even though I knew I shouldn't. I never told anyone that. I was afraid to talk about him to anyone in case they could tell I'd had a crush on him. I pretended I didn't really know him. It was easier that way. Seeing Wesley around has brought it back a lot harder than I was expecting. He's only a couple of years older than Chris was when he died. That's what I was trying to run away from when I went out to the deck on the ferry. Those memories. The guilt." She sat back and ran both hands over her eyes. "You must think I'm such a mess."

"No, I think you are exquisitely human, and that I am a very lucky man to have met you. I think you're probably exhausted from taking care of a lot of people and carrying a lot of worries all by yourself. But don't you see, you're not alone, and you don't have to be." A tender smile brushed his lips. "I think that we should pray for God to help you see how very loved and very precious you are. And then, after that, it's about time we finally have that interview."

SEVENTEEN

A phone was ringing—the loud, insistent noise shattering the last remnants of a deep sleep that had been all too short. Meg opened her eyes and blinked. Sunlight was streaming through her bedroom window. What time was it? Almost ten. She blinked. She couldn't remember the last time she'd slept in that late. The phone call went through voice mail.

She and Jack had talked into the early hours of the morning. His thoughtful questions peeled back the layers of her memory, bringing her thoughts and feelings about the Raincoat Killer out into the light.

Her hand brushed along the side of her neck. She'd never felt so listened to.

Picking up the phone, she noted that the missed call was from Rachel. In her voice mail, the young bride was irate and demanding, verging on hysterical. Apparently she'd just gone past the pavilion and noticed one of the windows had been boarded up. "I'm supposed to be getting married tonight! That's supposed to be where my reception is! I thought my fountain of flowers was arriving this morning. What are you going to do about it?"

What *was* she going to do about it?

Meg took a deep breath and let it out again. Then she called Alyssa Burne.

"I'm guessing you've heard everything that's happened recently from your husband and your father-in-law," Meg said. "I'm supposed to be co-ordinating Rachel and Wesley's wedding this evening. But I can't. I need to give myself time to heal and regroup, and dealing with this couple is killing me. Would you be willing to take it over? It's at sunset, followed by a reception at the pavilion."

"Absolutely." Alyssa's voice was professional, sympathetic and above all reassuring. "I'm happy to take it over. No problem."

Thank You, God.

"Everything is already arranged and ready to go. There's very little to do at this point, but just be available as a contact point. You'll have to check whether the pavilion window will be fixed, or if you're going to have to decorate over it somehow. You might also need to talk the bride and groom into doing their wedding photos inside the pavilion rather than on the beach depending on when the storm hits."

"You can count on me."

"Good. I'll email you all the details. I'll call the bride and groom, and also her grandmother in the nursing home who is covering all the bills, to tell them about the change in plans and give them your number. I'll also let all the suppliers know that you'll be the woman on location. If I can, I'll drop by the pavilion in a bit to check in too. Also, feel free to call me at any time today if you need anything, and I'll come right over."

"Don't worry. It will be fine. I'm sure of it."

Meg smiled. "Me too. Then maybe we can meet up next week and talk about how to work together in future. Honestly, there are more brides wanting to get married up here than I can handle. It would be wonderful to share some of that load."

She stared at the phone for a few moments after hanging up. Her shoulders felt lighter than they had in a long time.

Well, Lord, I hope trusting her was the right decision.

Then she called Rachel and kept it simple and short. She told the bride that she'd just gone through something traumatic, which she was sure Rachel would read about in the papers any moment now, and Alyssa was taking over the wedding.

The bride swore. "Today is my wedding day!"

"I know, and I'm sorry. I'm sure it will be absolutely fine."

"I'm going to sue you into the ground, you worthless piece of garbage."

Meg held the phone away from her ear and prayed for fifteen seconds before letting herself respond. "I'm sorry you feel that way. But I am positive Alyssa will do an amazing job. Everything is already set up exactly as you wanted it to be. You won't even notice the difference."

But Rachel was yelling so loudly Meg couldn't even get a word in edgewise. She winced. The young bride was hurling insults and slurs down the phone line like daggers. Meg had always known, in her heart, just how selfish and self-centered this bride could be. That self-centeredness had been present when she was a preteen in Meg's Sunday-school class and it had never gone away. It had almost been as if other people weren't actually real to her, but chess pieces to be moved around in the creation of her perfect wedding, her ideal life, just the way she wanted. "Rachel, please, a kid's in the hospital."

"Do I know him? No. I've never even met him. So what difference does that make? People get themselves hurt and end up in the hospital all the time! This is my wedding! My only wedding! Don't you get that? You stupid—"

Meg hung up.

Oh, Lord, please help this young couple. Help them heal from the wounds of their childhoods.

Help them see that real love isn't about grabbing or clutching on to who or what you want but in caring for the needs of others.

Meg tried Wesley, couldn't reach him and ended up leaving a message on his cell phone. Then she finished her phone calls, sorted her emails and got showered and dressed, before gathering the courage to leave her little sanctuary and go find Jack. Their conversation last night had been intimate. The kiss in the pavilion had been thrilling. It was as if yesterday had changed everything between them and yet left her with no idea of what he wanted to happen next.

Butterflies scurried around her heart and fluttered through her limbs. She liked him. She respected him. She was drawn to him emotionally in a way she'd never been drawn to anyone before. She didn't know what she wanted to happen next. But something inside her couldn't help smiling at the thought of seeing him.

The kitchen was spotless but empty. The dishes had been done and a fresh pot of coffee had been set up ready to be switched on. There was a note on the counter.

Hey, Sis,
Gone in to open the shop. Don't know what happened to Jack. He was gone when I woke

up. Took his stuff with him. Call me when
you get up. Love you.
Benji.

Gone? The butterflies in her stomach started
swirling faster, until she felt them forming into a
swarm. She knocked twice on the open basement
door, then went downstairs and walked through
the Benji's apartment. No one was there and Jack's
stuff truly was all gone. She called Jack's phone
and got his voice mail. Then she called her brother
at the store.

"Hey!" Benji's voice boomed. "You okay? Have
you seen the news? Jack posted his story early
this morning, and the internet jumped all over it."

She glanced through the empty living room.
"No, I haven't seen it. But it can wait. I think I
want to get out of here and be with people. You
okay if I come to the store and join you for lunch?"

"Absolutely. Don't you have a wedding on?"

"Not anymore. I decided to use my opt-out
clause in the contract and passed it onto Alyssa
Burne."

Benji whistled. "I'm so proud of you! Yeah,
come on over. We'll eat."

There was a heavy knocking at the door. "Great,
I'm on my way."

The knocking grew louder. She tucked her hair

behind her ears, slid her bag over her shoulder and reached for the door handle.

A bright light flashed. A camera clicked. A giant microphone was thrust into her face.

"*Impact News* from Toronto. Meg Duff, how do you respond to the charge you helped perpetrate a serial-killer fraud on the public?"

"Excuse me?" *A fraud?* What on earth was he on about? She shoved the microphone out of her face. "I have no idea what you're talking about." The so-called reporter was a freckled kid barely in his twenties. The photographer's face was totally hidden by the giant lens. Meg slammed the door and pushed past them. A black rental car was parked in the driveway behind her hatchback. "And get out of my driveway before I call the police."

The photographer kept snapping. The reporter smirked. "You are the same Meg Duff that was interviewed by Jack Brooks of *Torchlight News?*"

She didn't turn. She'd been a pro at ignoring tabloid reporters before this kid had even figured out how to hold a microphone. Had she been naive not to expect them to descend on her now? She yanked her car keys from her pocket. "I have no comment. I suggest you direct your questions to the police."

"Did you know that Toronto's chief of police

has repeatedly denounced Brooks as an attention seeker and a liar?"

The words hit her back like bullets. No, she didn't. But she wasn't about to tell some tabloid reporter that.

"Did you know the chief of police in Toronto called Brooks's story about the so-called Raincoat Killer nothing but a piece of imaginative fiction?"

The keys rattled in her hand.

"Did you help Brooks perpetrate that fiction with a series of stunts on Manitoulin Island?" The reporter's questions flew like machine-gun fire. "Did you try to convince the police that an old man's suicide was really murder? Did you trick a kid into dressing up like the so-called Raincoat Killer and attacking you on security camera?"

The camera kept flashing. Meg shoved the keys into the door so hard they nearly broke. "I will say this one last time. Get off my property or I'll call the police." She yanked the driver's door open.

The reporter grabbed the doorframe. "Did Brooks pay you to lie for him? Did he cook up the story about you being attacked on the ferry as a desperate attempt to save his career? Or are you just another victim of his hoax?"

The car door slammed inches away from his fingers. She pulled her phone from her pocket and dialed nine-one-one.

The reporter signaled at the photographer to fall

back. "No need to call the police. One last question, Ms. Duff, and we'll be gone." He leaned toward the window. "How much do you really trust Jack Brooks?"

The marina was busier than she'd seen it all season. Families crowded the beach. The water teemed with sailboats, Windsurfers and personal watercraft, despite the hint of dark clouds on the distant horizon. The radio said a major thunderstorm was coming, one of those bad summer tempests that pelted the ground and churned the water's surface like a pot on rolling boil.

Which wasn't a bad way to describe the emotional mess teeming inside her heart. The *Impact* reporters had jumped in their car and peeled away before nine-one-one dispatch had even put her through to the local police. She'd spoken to someone at the local police station, who'd then put her through to Detective Ravine. Ravine had offered to have a car swing by her house if the reporters came back. *If?* She'd gritted her teeth and asked the detective if he knew why a tabloid reporter would accuse Jack of perpetrating a hoax. He'd told her to ask Jack.

Which she would have done, if he hadn't left while she was sleeping.

She parked the car behind Benji's store. A familiar figure was sitting hunched at a picnic bench by the water, typing in a laptop while talking on the phone. Was Jack waiting for her? For Benji? Or had he just been looking for a place to sit and kill time? She took a deep breath and walked down the boardwalk toward him. His laptop snapped shut as she drew closer and his phone call ended. But even then, his head didn't turn toward her until she spoke his name.

"Hello, Jack."

He nodded, slowly, with just the glimmer of a smile on his lips that was far more sad than happy. "We need to talk."

"You bet we do. You moved out of my home in the middle of the night without even leaving a note. Then a tabloid reporter showed up banging on my door."

His elbows rested on the top of the picnic table. His shoulders sagged like those of a man twice his age. "It wasn't the middle of the night. It was quarter to six in the morning. I'd gotten through to my editor, Vince. My interview with you was about to go live on the website, and he made it pretty clear to me that considering the risk he was taking in running it, he wasn't about to also risk upsetting the publishers when they figured out I was staying with you. So I told him I'd move out immediately, before the article went live. You and your brother were still asleep. I figured I'd go find a coffee shop to sit in for a while, sort things out and explain it to you later. I'm sorry I didn't leave a note—it honestly didn't occur to me until you said it just now. Maybe I got into the habit of acting first and explaining later at work. Or I'm just too used to being on my own. Anyway, it was a snap decision, and I didn't know exactly where I was going."

A snap decision. Of course. From a man who was still all gut reactions and impulses.

Her arms snapped across her chest. "Your editor didn't have a problem with you bunking with my brother yesterday?"

"Yesterday, Vince was still hoping I'd somehow manage to wrangle an interview out of you."

She sucked in a breath.

"I didn't mean it like that." He dropped his head into his hands. "Look, I had no choice. The paper has a very strict policy about a reporter interviewing anyone he or she is in a personal relationship with. The only way around it would have been if I'd declared it as a potential conflict of interest right there on the page, and also gone through the necessary steps to clear it with the publishers first. There's an internal review process I would've had to go through, and it's not the kind of thing I could do without a lot of sober thought—not to mention, a lot of time to work things out." He shrugged. "It just seemed simpler to publish the story first and sort us out later."

She leaned her hands on the picnic table until her face was level with his. "What kind of personal relationship do we have, Jack?"

He shrugged. "I don't know anymore. I honestly don't. All I know is that I can't have this conversation right this second. Not after everything that happened yesterday. I need some time to figure everything out with work, talk to some friends and pray. Then I'll get back to you, and we'll see where we stand." He ran his hand over the back of his neck. "Otherwise I'll end up just impulsively blurting out the first thing I'm thinking, without taking the time to be sure. I'm sure you can appreciate that taking some breathing space makes sense right now."

Unbelievable. "So *now* you've decided it's time to start thinking things through? Now that I've got the tabloids banging down my door, my life has been threatened more times than I can count and an angry bride is threatening to sue me and ruin my business? This is when you decide to walk away?"

His jaw rolled slowly, as if his mouth were struggling to form words. "I told you the last time I tried to mix personal feelings for someone with an article I was working on, I nearly lost everything. I'm sorry that everything has changed since yesterday, but it has. Stuart's still unconscious in the hospital. You're now on the cover of my newspaper. There's a chance Ravine can talk the Toronto chief into reopening the murder cases on Krista, Eliza and Shelly. And yes, if my editor thinks it's going to be a whole lot easier to get the story taken seriously if I move out of your brother's basement apartment, it's worth it to help make sure a serial killer doesn't keep getting away with murder. Do you honestly think I wanted to have to choose between doing my job and spending time with you?"

"Don't you dare put that on me." Her voice rose. "I never asked you to push your way into my life, and I never asked you to choose between me and your job. And how secure is that job anyway? Why did some paparazzi tell me you're nothing but a disgraced reporter who's in trouble with the police for inventing a serial killer? He said the Raincoat Killer was denounced as a hoax. Is that true?"

His face fell. "I thought you trusted me."

"I thought I did too." Her head shook. "But you said yourself that a whole lot has changed since yesterday."

"The truth," Jack said, "is that three women died in Toronto, at the hands of what I believe to be the same killer. The truth is that while individual police whispered and gossiped off the record about there being a serial killer on the loose, the chief of police was unwilling to confirm that to the press or tell the public that. I thought lives were in danger. I wrote what I knew to be true. My editor made the call to run it and plastered it on the front page of our paper. Because when the police won't act, the press does. That's our job, to keep the police accountable and the public informed. The chief of police was publicly humiliated, and rather than admitting his detectives' conclusions might in fact be wrong he threw me under the bus to save his career, denouncing me in a press conference. The publisher wanted me fired. The editor suggested I take a few days off. I'm not the type of man who likes sitting around doing nothing, so because I thought there could be a Manitoulin Island connection to the killer I hopped on a bus and came up here. Then I met you, and everything changed."

His eyes fixed back on hers. Piercing. Unflinching. Burning with an intensity that made her suddenly gasp for breath. "I have never once lied to you, Meg, and I never will. Do you honestly not know what I think about you? How I feel about you? You are the most beautiful, brave, extraordinary person I've ever met in my life, and when I'm around you, I want to do everything in my power to take care of you and protect you."

A long breath left her body. "I don't believe you ever knowingly lied to me. I still want to trust you. But ever since you walked into my life, my world has fallen apart. You say you want to protect me? What if you're the only reason my life is now in danger?"

EIGHTEEN

He watched in disbelief as a cold, determined glint of gray moved through the blue of her eyes. What was she saying? That everything she'd been through was somehow his fault?

He leaned forward. "Look, I don't know what that tabloid reporter told you, but all I have done since meeting you is try to keep you safe. You've got to know that."

She sighed. Resignation seemed to ripple through her body. Then she sat down opposite him. "I know that's what you believe, Jack. But what if you're wrong? What if you're the one the killer has been after all this time, not me? You're the one who baited him with a big cover story. You think the Raincoat Killer came up here, after me, because of some flyers you saw at the crime scenes. But what if the killer saw your story and followed you up here? What if the killer attacked me on the ferry because he saw you talking to me? What if the Raincoat Killer has been after you all this time and I'm just a stranger that got caught in the cross fire? What if your determination to get that interview from me was the only thing that has put my life in danger?"

He blinked. She couldn't be serious. How could she turn everything around in her head like this? Reject him as her hero and recast him as an unwitting villain? "That's not what my gut instinct is telling me."

"All your 'gut instinct' has done so far is hurt me."

He felt the color drain from his face. "Meg. You can't mean that." But even as he said it, he could see from the tears threatening her eyes that she meant every word. *Oh Lord, just how much hurt have I caused her?*

"Then answer me this, Jack, if you hadn't wanted an interview from me, would you have walked up to me on the ferry? Would you have stayed with my brother? Would you ever have stuck around in my life after we made it to shore?"

He opened his mouth, but words failed him.

Unrelenting eyes searched his face. "If I hadn't trusted you last night, Jack, if I hadn't opened up to you, told you my secrets, my feelings, my fears, would you still have run out of my life this morning?"

"Do you really want me to answer that?" He reached for her. His fingers brushed the back of her hand. His voice was so soft it was almost a whisper. "I care about you. You've got to know that. Regardless of the fact that I wanted to interview you. You're extraordinary to me."

Then as he watched, something broke inside her eyes. Her shoulders heaved. "But you're leaving anyway. So it's best we just say goodbye and not try to drag this out any further than it already has been."

Just like that, he felt the last glimmer of hope die in his chest, leaving nothing but an empty, heavy ache. What had he hoped for actually? That she would understand? That she wouldn't be hurt? She was right that he had to leave—he'd been fooling himself to think that she'd want him to come back someday. It's not like he was in any position to ask her to wait for him.

"You know it's not personal, right?" he asked. "This whole thing has just gotten too murky professionally. What else would you have me do? March into my editor's office and tell him that I need to keep seeing you—even though this story is so explosive right now that one wrong move could end both my career and his? What reason could I give him? Because you're my friend? Because you're someone I'm attracted to? Because you're someone who I'd hope to be in a real relationship with one day if you weren't so determinedly convinced I would only end up hurting you? This Raincoat Killer is not just going to sit around waiting while we figure out how we feel. I can't just be floating around in an uncertain relationship, a no-man's land, with someone I'm writing about. I can't just keep spending time with you while keeping my emotional distance either. Maybe I could pretend to on the outside, but not in how I feel."

His phone began to ring. *Simon.* He pressed the button to send the call to voice mail.

She stood. "Where are you going to go?"

"Home. Back to Toronto. I'm leaving on the afternoon ferry. My boss wants to meet up for coffee tonight. The newspaper is really getting behind this story now. We're going to dig our heels in, write a whole series of articles and really push the chief of police to seriously reexamine this case." His phone chirped. Simon was calling back. He hit voice mail again.

"Well, congratulations, then, I guess. Good luck."

"Thanks."

"Please try to stay safe."

"I will." He gritted his teeth and stared at the clouds on the edge of the horizon, almost afraid of what he'd see if he looked in her eyes. "You too."

"Goodbye, Jack." She turned and walked down the boardwalk.

He breathed in a deep agonized breath as he

heard a muffled sound of a sob leaving her throat. *Well, Lord. It looks like I messed that up.*

More ringing. The call went through to voice mail for a third time. He wasn't sure he was ready to talk to his friend right now.

Jack had called the social worker earlier that morning to see if he'd had any luck showing around the pictures he'd sent. Simon hadn't. But then Jack somehow ended up telling him about Meg. Everything about Meg. From what they'd survived together, to how much he admired and esteemed her. Even that he'd kissed her. He'd expected Simon to offer to pray for him or recommend a Bible verse. Instead there'd been a long pause on the other end of the phone, followed by six simple words that had knocked the air from Jack's lungs faster than a physical blow: "Well, Jack, do you love her?"

He hadn't known what to say. Did he? Even if he did, what could he possibly do about it? He had felt her heart turning so slowly toward his with every glance, every touch and every conversation. But it would take time for anything deeper to grow. Time he simply didn't have.

The phone started ringing a fourth time. "Hey, Simon. What's up?"

"Jack. We got a hit on one of the pictures. It's not a very nice one, but it's solid."

Well, considering the kind of places Simon and

his social-work colleagues were often called into, Jack had hardly expected "nice." He grabbed a pen. "What've you got?"

Simon took a breath. "Someone from our community garden recognized Eliza Penn, the florist who was run over by a car. She used to drop by the project last summer to help tend plants and pull weeds. Some of the other volunteers began to suspect Eliza's boyfriend was controlling and abusive. He'd show up and demand she leave with him. A couple of people heard him yelling insults at her. People noticed bruises that she tried to explain away with pretty unconvincing excuses. Typical signs of domestic violence."

"This nasty piece of work got a name?"

"Duncan Kitts. My colleague recognized the picture, and the name."

Jack sucked in a breath. The tall, bald best man. The one Meg had a bad feeling about from the start. Why wasn't he surprised?

"Our staff and volunteers encouraged her to get help," Simon continued. "They offered to go with her to the police and to help her get a restraining order. But Eliza kept insisting she was fine and that she was going to break up with him."

Jack nodded. The story was heartbreaking and one he'd heard too many times before. "Guess he wasn't ready to let her go."

"One of my colleagues tried to keep in touch

with Eliza after the project wrapped up, but she'd moved out of her apartment and changed her phone number. They figured she was just trying to get away from Duncan. After she died, my colleagues went to the police with their suspicions, obviously, but I don't know if anyone ever questioned the guy, or even considered him a suspect in the other murders."

"They probably realized he had an ironclad alibi, because he'd been up North in the Arctic at the time." Jack would have almost laughed if it hadn't been so deadly serious.

Here the police had tried to convince him the murders had been either copycat crimes or sick coincidences because witnesses couldn't agree on how tall the Raincoat Killer was. Well, what if there hadn't just been one? Someone had hired Kenny—if it had been Duncan, then perhaps he'd deliberately arranged for the teenager to attack at a time when Duncan himself would have an alibi. And if Duncan could have hired Kenny to pretend to be a killer, who's to say he didn't hire someone to kill Krista and Eliza while he was in the Arctic? If so, had he also hired someone to kill Shelly, or had Duncan done that one himself?

"Anyway, that's all I got," Simon said. "Hope it helps. By the way, I read your cover story in the paper today. Solid stuff. I'm praying."

"Thanks, man. Don't stop."

Jack hung up and called Benji. "Hey, it's Jack. Don't hang up."

"I'm listening," Benji said.

Thank You, God. "I don't know if we're cool or not. But I've just heard that the best man from Meg's wedding, Duncan, has a history of beating on women. Can you call her and let her know to stay away from him?"

There was a pause. "Okay," Benji said. "I'll tell her. She's not doing the wedding now, so she probably won't see him. But I have. He just left my store not ten minutes ago. He wanted to return some of the supplies they'd bought yesterday, plus get some maps of the area. Told me he'd bought out the yacht rental from the bride and groom and was off to do some solo sailing."

Duncan was going to head off on the honeymoon yacht without the happy couple? "Why?"

"I don't know. But I do know he was looking to fill up a jerry can with extra gasoline."

This picture was looking worse by the moment. Whether or not Duncan was the person who'd hired Kenny, making a quick escape from the island didn't make him look innocent.

"I hear you and Meg talked," Benji added.

That was one word for it. "Yeah, and I'm sorry. I didn't want things to play out this way."

"Then don't. Fix it."

Right. Fix it. And how was he supposed to do that? "Just keep her safe, okay?"

"Always."

Jack hung up. Now what? As much as he'd love to call Vince and fill him in on the news about Duncan, there was no way he was going to let a potential killer walk the island without contacting the police first. He slid Detective Ravine's card from the bag. It rang through to voice mail. He tried again.

"Hello?" The voice was gruff and sounded only partially awake.

"Detective Ravine. Hi. It's Jack Brooks. You told me to call you if I had any serious leads, and I wasn't about to trust this to a general dispatcher."

"What have you got?"

"Duncan Kitts used to date Eliza Penn, the Raincoat Killer's second victim. He also used to beat her. Kitts was on the ferry when Meg was attacked and is also the best man in the wedding she was planning for this weekend."

There was a long pause. "I'm sorry, the name doesn't ring a bell. Which I must admit is worrying. While I wasn't lead investigator on Penn's hit-and-run, I'd like to think I'd remember if she had a boyfriend."

"They'd apparently broken up and he had a solid alibi at the time, so the police may not have looked into it too deeply. But once I realized someone hired Kenny to pretend to be the Raincoat Killer, it wasn't that big a stretch to realize he could have hired someone to kill Eliza Penn too."

"Do you have evidence of any of this? Any hard proof he committed any kind of crime?"

"No, sir. Just secondhand news from someone I trust plus a really solid hunch."

"Sadly, I can't just bring him in for questioning based purely on your hunch." Ravine paused. "Is there any evidence he has even committed a crime? Anything I can charge him with? Let me guess. No?" Another sigh. Longer and louder, like a southerly wind trying to decide whether to whip up into a storm. "I'll check with my team back in Toronto and see whether they did bother to investigate Duncan Kitts when the case first broke. He might have a record, something I can use as an excuse to have him brought in for questioning. In the meantime, we can use his name to press Kenny Smythe hard and see if that's enough to bluff him into thinking we have something more. It might work."

"With all due respect," Jack said, "there might not be time for that. He's got a boat in the marina, fully stocked with extra fuel, and apparently he's going to head off sailing. If he does, he'll disappear before Kenny Smythe can tell you anything, and I'm guessing that once it leaves, island police are hardly going to dispatch a fleet of boats to search the Great Lakes and Saint Lawrence for him."

"Probably not." Another pause, longer this time. "But please realize, Mr. Brooks, the police have procedures for things like this. While your instincts may be strong about this guy, the actual hard evidence I could present to a judge in order to get a warrant for his arrest is pretty flimsy. The police can't charge down the beach to stop this guy, just because I heard through the grapevine he used to beat his girlfriend."

"Maybe not." Jack slung his bag over his shoulder and started down the boardwalk. "But I can."

Thick plywood covered the broken glass window where Meg had watched a boy nearly lose his life. But the second-story door to the pavilion was open, and she could see someone moving inside. Alyssa setting up for the wedding, probably. Or the deliverymen dropping off Rachel's flower fountain. She climbed the wrought-iron stairs.

Her phone rang with Benji's ring tone. She pulled the phone from her pocket and accidentally knocked it to voice mail.

It was only then she realized she'd also somehow missed two texts from Rachel.

You around? Can you talk?
Call me. It's important.

Really? What did the self-important bride want to talk to her about now? If it was complaining about Alyssa, she wasn't interested in hearing it. The wedding had been so well organized it would run without a planner at this point.

Torn and twisted police tape lay discarded at the top of the stairs. Shards of broken glass still clung to the very edges of the window frame. She pushed the door open. The pavilion was empty. Her feet echoed across the wooden floor. Whoever she thought she'd spotted in the window earlier was now nowhere to be seen.

She ignored Rachel's texts and called Benji.

He answered even before it could ring once. "Hey. Where are you?"

"At the pavilion." The tables and chairs had been pushed back against the wall. Under the far window sat the ornate, flowered fountain Rachel had insisted on. It was even larger in person than she'd expected. "I just needed a walk. You ready for lunch?"

"Are you with anyone right now?" There was a protective edge to her brother's voice, as though he was concerned but trying not to let it show.

"No, I'm alone." She crossed over to the kitchen and stepped inside. Catering trays were already laid out for the reception. "Why? Everything okay?"

"I'm on my way over. I'll meet you there in fifteen."

She heard a door slam shut. She spun. A chill ran down her spine. There was no one there.

"Just meet me outside," Benji said. "If you see Duncan, the best-man guy, just steer clear of him. Okay?"

"Absolutely." She walked back through into the pavilion, just in time to see a shadow disappear down the stairs. "Why? Is everything okay?"

"Not really, no." There was the jangle of Benji's store door closing. "We'll talk when I see you. Just stay away from him, okay? I'm on my way now."

"Okay." She reached for the door handle, stepped outside and froze.

Duncan was standing on the steps in front of her.

NINETEEN

"Meg?" Her brother's voice crackled in her ear.

Duncan's bulk blocked the stairs. His eyes opened wide, as though he was more surprised at seeing her than she was of him. One huge fist gripped the railing. The other shoved a smartphone back into his pocket. She didn't know why her brother had warned her to stay away from Duncan, but she wasn't sure she needed a reason.

She forced a cheerful smile onto her lips. "Hi, Duncan!" Her tone was light and her voice was loud. "I didn't expect to see you here today."

"He's there?" Benji's voice was so loud she was certain Duncan could hear it too.

"I'm just talking to Duncan."

"I'm on my way."

For a second she could hear the sound of Benji running. Then the phone went dead. She slipped it back into her jeans. Then she glanced back up at Duncan. He was easily twice her size. A solid mass of muscle and aggression. His eyes narrowed.

Her smile didn't falter. "Excuse me, Duncan. I'm just heading down the stairs."

He didn't exactly step back, but making herself as small as possible, she squeezed past him anyway. His weight pressed against her, nearly pushing her into the railing. She kept going. Her phone started ringing again. She didn't answer it.

"Who were you talking to?" Duncan's voice sounded close behind her. He was following.

"My brother."

He was walking so closely behind her that he was nearly pushing her down the stairs. "You were talking about me, weren't you?

She didn't answer. Just a few more feet and she'd be out on the beach. Her foot hit the boardwalk. His hand grabbed her elbow.

"I said, were you talking to him about me?" His grip tightened. He twisted her arm behind her back, just subtly enough that no one passing by would see.

"Hey! Duncan Kitts!" Jack pelted down the boardwalk. The microphone of his voice recorder was stuck out in front of him like a weapon. "I'm Jack Brooks, reporter from *Torchlight News* in Toronto. Did you hire Kenny Smythe to pretend to be the Raincoat Killer?"

Duncan let go of her arm. "What is this?" His voice came out as a growl.

Jack's eyes met hers for a fraction of a second,

as solid and serious as a bullet. *What on earth is he doing?* He pushed the microphone deeper into Duncan's face. His voice rose until it was almost a shout. "Did you hire Kenny Smythe to play the part to give yourself an alibi?"

Duncan snorted. "No comment." His hand shot out, smacking Jack in the shoulder and shoving him back several feet before turning to walk away.

Meg glanced at Jack. Her hand reached out for his.

"Thank you," she said. "I'm so grateful you were here. What's going on?"

But Jack brushed right past her, as if she hadn't even spoken. He followed Duncan down the boardwalk. "Mr. Kitts, how do you answer charges that you used to terrorize Eliza Penn?" His voice rang loudly through the air. "Did you pay someone to kill your former girlfriend?" Duncan stopped. He turned. His hands clenched at his side. Jack stepped up to him and stood toe-to-toe with a man almost twice his width. "Mr. Kitts, did you shoot local teenager Stuart Smythe? Did you murder Mr. McCarthy? Did you attack Meg Duff?"

"Get out of my way." Duncan snatched the voice recorder from Jack's hand and threw it to the ground. Then he stomped on it. But Jack stood firm. Courage blazed in his eyes with a fire that set her heart alight and stole the breath from her lungs. A crowd of spectators was forming around them now, held back in near silence by the tension that filled the air around them. Families led their children away down the beach. People were pulling out their phones to record what was taking place.

A wide smile spread across Jack's face. "Do you enjoy trying to frighten men too, Mr. Kitts? Or do you just prefer hurting women?"

The motion was swift, violent and merciless as Duncan drove his fist into Jack's jaw. The sucker punch snapped Jack's neck back. Meg gripped the bottom of the railing. Prayers poured from her lips. What was wrong with Jack? Why was he baiting Duncan like this? Did the man never even stop to think before he acted? He was putting himself in danger, and for what? Duncan's fists flew toward him again, relentlessly trying to beat Jack into the boardwalk. Jack swerved and rolled to avoid the blows but didn't once strike back.

She had to help him. Meg grabbed her phone. The sound of sirens filled the air. The police were already on their way. Some of the larger men in the crowd had jumped into the fray now, pulling Duncan off Jack.

Her phone started ringing. She pressed a finger to her ear. "Hello?"

"Oh, Meg!" It was Rachel, her voice breathless and weepy. In all the time she'd known Rachel, Meg hadn't once known her to come even close to crying. "I'm so glad I reached you. I'm so sorry for what I said before." Meg hadn't known her to apologize either, for that matter.

What could possibly have happened? "I'm here. What's wrong? Are you okay?"

A burst of sobs was her only response.

"Hang on," Meg said, "I'm going somewhere quieter."

Jack was sitting on the boardwalk with his head in his hands. Everything in her heart ached to run to him. But everything she'd seen in the last five minutes made it clear why she couldn't. Jack had just gone out of his way to pick a fight with Duncan, when he could have just let the man go on his way. Yes, he'd been there and stepped in when she needed him, and maybe because he'd known why Benji had warned her to stay away from the groomsman. But her brother was only moments away. And once Duncan had walked away, she had been safe, and yet Jack had run right past Meg, brushing her off, as he charged headlong into danger, for no apparent reason other than presumably the urging of his own gut instinct. Once again, she'd been left on the sidelines, this time watching the man she cared about get hurt and holding her breath as a monster twice Jack's size tried to pound him into the ground.

This had to stop. She had to let him go. This

wasn't the kind of man she could let herself love, or entrust her life and future to.

No matter how desperately she wanted to.

Meg walked around to the other side of the pavilion, holding her phone to her ear. "Okay. I'm back. Are you still there?"

"Yes." Rachel sniffed. "Wesley left me."

"He did what?"

"He got cold feet, I guess. I don't know what happened! He seemed fine last night, but then he just disappeared. Alyssa couldn't reach him at all this morning. Duncan said he hadn't seen him all day. Fiona went to the hotel and they said he'd checked out. He didn't even leave me a note."

Meg's heart sank. She'd known Wesley was nervous. She'd thought talking to her brother might help. Was this her fault? Should she have tried contacting him last night after the rehearsal to see if he was okay? "I'm so, so sorry."

"I need to talk to someone. Where are you?"

"At the marina. Behind the pavilion."

"Please," Rachel said. "I literally have no one else to talk to. Alyssa is sweet, but she doesn't know me. Fiona can't possibly handle something like this. I can't tell my grandmother. Not after all the money she's spent on this wedding."

It was just as well that Rachel didn't mention wanting to confide in the best man—Duncan wouldn't be much use to her since the police were hauling him off. "Where are you?"

"I'm on the yacht we rented at the marina."

So, less than five minutes' walk from where she stood. "Okay. I'll be there in a moment."

"Thank you!"

"No problem. Just hang on. I'll see you in a second." Meg hung up and headed for the docks. The fight between Duncan and Jack had ended, but a mess of people still stood around in front of the beach. She counted four cop cars and two paramedics. She couldn't see Jack. She couldn't see Benji either. She dialed his cell phone. It went through to voice mail.

"Hey, Benji. It's me. I'm guessing you caught some of the big fight on the beach. I don't know what happened. Duncan was intimidating me. Jack confronted him and then practically chased him down the boardwalk. It was kind of heroic at first—until it got out of hand." Her feet echoed along the dock. "Anyway, just wanted to let you know I was heading to meet Rachel on the yacht. I know I said I was finished with this wedding, but apparently we now have a runaway groom and a jilted bride. Rachel's a mess and she wants someone to talk to. Come meet me there and we'll head for food. Bye."

She hung up the phone and stepped up on the small gangplank.

The deck was deserted.

"Hello?"

"Meg?" Rachel's voice drifted through the open hatch. "Down here."

"Okay." She climbed down the narrow flight of stairs into a surprisingly large kitchen. A boat rental like this must have cost thousands.

An arm wrapped around her neck before she could even scream. Her hands scratched desperately at the fabric of the orange raincoat. A gloved hand locked over her mouth while a knee hit the small of her back, forcing her to the floor. *Lord, save me—*

Then, mercifully, she felt the heavy blanket of unconsciousness sweep over her mind.

TWENTY

Jack sat on a bench and watched as the yacht disappeared like a speck on the horizon.

There went Duncan's getaway vehicle.

"Well, that was either the bravest or the most foolish thing I've ever seen." Benji pressed a bottle of water into his hands. "And that's saying a lot coming from me."

"Trust me, it wasn't my preferred option." Jack pressed the cold bottle against his aching jaw. "But I don't know what other choice there was. I had a credible source telling me that Duncan beat and threatened Eliza Penn. He might very well be responsible for her murder. You told me he was about to board a boat. The police needed time to gather evidence to charge him with murder…but an assault charge was something they could arrest him for right away. This way, the police are able to hold him for twenty-four hours and hopefully keep him in custody long enough to get enough evidence to charge him with something better, or at least use him to rattle a confession out of Kenny Smythe." He grinned. "All I was really doing was trying to avoid getting punched, and trying not to punch him back." Last thing he wanted was an assault charge of his own. "I was just trying to stall him long enough for the police to get here."

Benji sat down. His eyes ran down the beach. "You seen my sister?"

"Yeah. She was by the pavilion just a few minutes ago. She was on the phone."

Benji reached into his pocket. He made a face at the screen and then called voice mail. "She left a message." He listened a moment, then chuckled. "She thinks your actions were heroic—at first, anyway. Though she does say it got out of hand. Doesn't know why you picked a fight with Duncan, though, does she?"

Jack shook his head. He didn't even want to guess how his actions must have looked from her perspective, but he'd hardly had time to explain.

"Meg says she's with Rachel on the yacht." Benji's forehead wrinkled. "And I don't see the boat."

The nerves at the back of Jack's neck snapped to attention. "I'm pretty sure I just watched that boat pull out of the marina."

Benji pushed a button on his phone and listened to it ring. "She's not answering her phone. Plus, Meg's message said that Wesley had done a runner and called off the wedding. So why would Rachel and Meg take the boat out alone?"

Getting dumped on her wedding day could easily leave Rachel distressed and irrational enough to drive off into a storm. But why wouldn't Meg try and stop her?

An ugly suspicion began to drip down the back of Jack's spine, pooling in the bottom of his gut. If Duncan was the Raincoat Killer, he hadn't acted alone. What if his accomplice was on the island? It would certainly explain how the killer had managed to lock them into McCarthy's garage so easily—one person securing each exit to make sure they were shut in with no escape.

His mind spun. All this time Meg had been convinced that Wesley couldn't be the Raincoat Killer. But what if Duncan had pressured him or bribed him into being an accomplice? Surely there was no one with a bigger motive to make Meg suffer than Wesley. What if he'd never forgiven her and Benji for Chris's accident?

Jack frowned. No, that theory didn't quite hold water. It was Rachel who'd asked Meg to meet her at the boat, and not Wesley. Was Rachel somehow trapped under Duncan's thumb? She might not even know he'd been arrested. Was the boat Rachel's getaway plan to escape from Duncan and her fiancé?

Or had Wesley forced Rachel to lure Meg onto

that boat? Maybe it had all been a ruse, and Wesley hadn't cancelled the wedding after all.

Benji dialed his sister again. This time it went straight through to voice mail. "Something's wrong if she's sailed out of cell-phone range. She wouldn't leave the harbor without telling me, and no self-respecting islander would head out onto Lake Huron with a major storm brewing."

The sick feeling in Jack's stomach grew. "Let's say we wanted to find her. What are the odds of getting a police boat or six to search Lake Huron for her?"

"Slim." Benji's eyes were grim. "The island doesn't have that big a police force, and they're unlikely to dispatch rescue boats without a really good reason to believe someone's in immediate danger." He stood and stared out to the horizon. "Don't get me wrong, I'll call them, and I'll use everything in my power to convince them to find her. But we're talking about finding one boat, somewhere in one of the world's largest lakes. Even if we can persuade them to send out a police boat, into a killer storm, based on not much more than a hunch, they'll need eyes in the sky to find her."

The dark, gathering clouds filled Jack's eyes. The thought of Meg in danger gripped his chest so tightly he could barely breathe. When Duncan had been arrested, Jack actually believed the Raincoat Killer's reign of terror could finally be over.

Now it seemed the nightmare was only beginning.

The room swayed gently underneath Meg's body. She opened her eyes with a start and gasped hard as her hands leapt to her throat. But there was no one there. She was very much alone, lying on a single bunk, in a small, sparse cabin. Dark gray clouds filled the window above her. Tears flooded her eyes. Praying silently, she thanked God that she was alive. But what had happened to Rachel?

She stood slowly and tried the cabin door. It was locked. She twisted the handle hard and threw her weight against the door, but it held solid. For a moment the urge to bang on the door with both hands and scream until she was hoarse raged inside her. But she batted it down, breathed deep and forced her pulse to settle. There was no telling what and who was on the other side of the door, and if she wanted to make it out of here in one piece she had to think. Logic, planning and order had always been her greatest allies. She wasn't about to abandon them now.

Okay, now what? Her eyes scanned the room. The narrow space was no larger than a closet. The small bunk was bolted to the wall, and it was bare except for a foam mattress. There was no other furniture. This was what they called a junior cabin. But from where she stood, it felt like a jail cell.

And nobody knew she was here. The singular thought filled her mind afresh with fear. She closed her eyes tightly and counted backward from twenty, until she felt her spirit calm enough to find the words to pray. *Well, Lord, you know how I always said I wanted to work on my panic attacks? It looks like I'm getting a crash course. Please don't leave me now. Help me remember whatever happens next, it is well with my soul.* Then her eyes opened as she checked her clothing. Her phone and wallet were gone. But she didn't seem hurt and she was still fully clothed. That was something at least.

She climbed onto the bed and looked out the window. The shoreline was disappearing in the distance. The window glass wouldn't budge under her fingers. But just as despair threatened to slip back into her soul, a brilliant rainbow swept across the sky above her. Someone was parasailing. She gasped. Why would anyone risk their life parasailing with a storm on the horizon? The figure hung underneath the parachute, silhouetted against the sky, his towrope disappearing out of her view. Any moment now the rain would fall, forcing him back to shore. But what if she could get him a message before then?

She pulled off her jacket, held it completely over the window and then pulled it back quickly. Up went the jacket and down again quickly, twice more. She repeated the sequence slowly, then once more quickly again. Three short, three long, three short. Three short, three long, three short. Morse code for *SOS. Help. Help. Help.*

A door flew open behind her with such force she heard the wood slam against the wall. A hooded figure yanked her back. A blow knocked Meg down onto the bed. Gloved hands reached for her throat. She kicked out hard. Her own screams filled her ears. Then the blackness swept over her again.

Thunder crashed, followed by the gentle patter of rain falling above her. Something soft and wet brushed against her forehead. Her eyes fluttered open. A tall figure in a black wet suit was towering over her. She struggled to move, but her hands were bound tight behind her back. A scream tried to escape her throat, only to be lost in the folds of the gag tied over her mouth.

"Meg. It's okay. You're okay. It's me." Jack pulled off his face mask. The tender warmth of his voice brushed over her skin, calming the panic inside her. "Now lie still. I'm going to free your hands." Her body relaxed as she turned her back toward him. One strong hand held hers in place.

There was a quick flick of motion behind her. Then she felt his fingers brush against her bare skin as the bonds fell away. "Now roll back," he whispered, "and I'll remove your gag."

How was he here? How had he found her? How long had she even been out? She closed her eyes and forced the clamoring in her mind to still. He was here. Jack was here and she was safe. The answers would come. Right now that was all that she needed to know.

She let his hands guide her body while her fingers enjoyed the feeling of stretching again and her eyes adjusted to the darkness. The pane was gone from the window, leaving nothing but an empty hole through which the rain now fell, covering the room and their bodies with a thin, wet mist. The sky was dark with the unnaturally gray haze of a late-afternoon storm. A small knife flashed in Jack's hands.

He eased the gag back from her mouth. His fingers brushed up against her cheek as he cradled her face in his hands. "The knots on this thing are pretty vicious, so I'm going to cut it off. Okay? I'm sorry for not removing it first. But I needed to be sure you'd calmed down enough that you weren't about to panic or scream. I don't want anyone knowing I'm onboard until we're ready to make a run for it."

Her eyes looked up into his. She nodded. There

was the quick brush of something cold against her jaw. And then her mouth was free. She gasped. A cleansing breath filled her lungs. And then—

She felt his lips on hers. Kissing her deeply. Gently. Pulling her into his arms. Surrounding her with his strength. Her hands slid around his neck, running through his wet hair. Allowing themselves just one brief moment, before he pulled back, just enough to let his voice brush against her ear. "I'm so sorry I left. I should have never left you alone."

"It's okay. You're here now."

"Are you hurt?" His fingers slid along her throat. "You looked bruised."

She shivered as he brushed her tender skin. "I was choked. Twice. They were wearing a raincoat." Her head fell against his shoulder. "I'm so glad you found me. How did you know where I was?"

"Benji told me you were on the yacht, but by the time I realized you could be in danger, the boat had already left the harbor. I didn't know how I was going to find you, until your brother suggested we get eyes in the sky."

"That was you on the parasail?"

He nodded. "Benji was driving the speedboat. He knows the shore and the shoals. He's hidden in an inlet not far from here."

She could guess which boat it was too. It was tiny, fast and sent chills of fear through her heart whenever Benji drove it. And Jack had talked him into going out on it, around the shoals, with a storm coming. "That was a pretty gutsy move." Not to mention courageous. "How long have I been gone?"

"Over an hour. I'm sorry we didn't come sooner, but your life is too valuable, to both of us, to risk by dashing off impulsively. It took some time to figure out what we were going to do, and how to do it safely." His fingers brushed along her bare arms and down along her tingling palms. Rain flicked at her face through the open window. Was this the same man she'd seen run unthinkingly down the boardwalk after a huge, angry beast of a man?

"Why did you chase Duncan down the beach?"

"It was the only option I had to make sure he didn't escape justice by slipping on a boat. This boat, in fact. I found a connection between Duncan and the Raincoat Killer's second victim. Eliza Penn. They were in an abusive relationship and he threatened her life. But the police didn't have enough evidence to arrest him, and he was about to leave the island."

Suddenly it all made sense. "So you stepped in and did what it took to make sure the police took him into custody before he could hurt anyone else."

"Pretty much. Plus, now they can hold him

awhile for assaulting me. Hopefully long enough to get Kenny to crack and tell the police Duncan was the one who hired him. It all makes sense. Or at least it did until someone kidnapped you." He pulled her closer. "When I realized the Raincoat Killer might have hired Kenny Smythe to wear the coat for him, it hit me that Duncan might have gotten someone else to kill Eliza for him while he was in the Arctic. I don't know how—or even if— the first victim, Krista Hooper, fits into all this. But Duncan definitely has the right height and build for the suspect in the third murder, Shelly Day, and we know he was back from the Arctic by then. I know you don't want to believe that Wesley could be involved, but I think we should at least face the possibility that Rachel lied to you about Wesley leaving and that he forced her to lure you onto the boat."

"Wesley seemed so shy and nervous." She shivered. "I still don't want to believe he'd hurt anybody."

"Wesley was strapped for cash after his parents died. Rachel's the only heir of a very wealthy, elderly woman. She's worth a lot of money when her grandmother eventually passes. People have killed for far less."

She leaned back deeper into the safety of Jack's arms. "Please tell me the police are coming."

A flash of lightning shone through the open

window, casting Jack's face in shades of sepia-brown and shadow. "No. Trust me, Benji and I tried hard to convince them to send a boat. But even with Duncan's arrest, the evidence linking him and Wesley to the Raincoat Killer was tenuous at best. Benji tried reaching the police on the radio when we saw you signaling for help. But we're too far from a cell tower and he couldn't reach anyone on a radio. We didn't dare head back to civilization and risk losing sight of you."

The rain was falling steadily now, pounding on the deck, nipping at their bodies. Thunder echoed in the distance. The storm was still small enough to boat in, but it wouldn't last that way for long.

"The only way this boat is going to survive the storm is if we find shore and drop anchor," she said.

"The boat is inching along at a crawl. I was able to outswim it no problem. I slipped onto the back and jimmied your window open without anyone noticing. They're lucky they haven't hit a shoal yet. The good news is that we're not that far offshore. Soon we'll be close enough to risk jumping out and swimming to Benji and his boat."

She nodded. "But we can't leave Rachel."

"You're asking me to risk your life in order to save hers?"

"I am."

His hand cradled her face again as his lips

slipped over her skin. Then he unclipped a walkie-talkie from his belt and pressed it into her hands. "It'll go like this. You slip out the window and onto the deck. Count backward in your head from a hundred and if you don't see me coming by the time you get to 'one,' jump overboard, swim to shore and call Benji. If you hear me shouting or you think Wesley spots you, don't wait, just swim. But don't use the walkie-talkie until you're ready to swim, otherwise Benji said the feedback could be loud enough to alert them something's up."

She clipped the walkie-talkie to her belt. "What about you?"

He sighed and ran his hand over the back of his head. "I'm going to try to get through this door and find Rachel. But I'm only searching the cabins down here and I'm not about to go up on deck and risk running into Wesley. Even if I do find Rachel, I might not be able to convince her to leave him. There's no way to knowing what lies he might have told her. My goal is to get both of us out there safely, not jump into a fight with a killer. If I can't find her, we go without her. Once we find Benji, we'll head back to within radio range and pray the police will be able to get to her in time to keep her safe." He stood. "Agreed?"

"Agreed." She took a deep breath. "And thank you. I—"

The cabin door flew open with a crash. The

Raincoat Killer stood in the doorway, his face fully hidden in the deep folds of the hood. An orange raincoat enveloped his body. A hunting rifle was held steady in his leather-gloved hands. Even if she or Jack managed to knock the barrel away from him, if the killer let off a single blast at this range, it would spray the tiny cabin with so much shrapnel, there was no way either of them would make it out alive.

"Wesley! Stop!" Jack stepped in front of Meg, shielding her with his body. "I know you love Rachel. I know you don't want her to get hurt. Let Meg and Rachel go. We can settle this, just the two of us."

Meg's breath caught in her throat. Her heart ached for Jack, for his courage, his strength. All this time she had wanted to keep him safe. But he didn't need her protection. He deserved her respect. The killer's finger tensed on the trigger.

Jack's hands rose, but when he spoke it was with a steady calm that sent chills up Meg's spine. "What do you want, Wesley? Revenge? Freedom? Duncan has been arrested. You think he's not going to tell the police it was you who killed Krista and Eliza? It's not too late to turn yourself in, cut a deal and tell the police that Duncan was behind it all. You were just doing what he told you to, right? Because he frightened you, or threatened you, or paid you off somehow? We can tell people that. Just put down that gun, and you and I can go sit somewhere quiet and talk. I'll give you all the time in the world to tell your story and I'll get it out to the media. I'll make sure everyone hears your side of the story. Please, for Rachel. Let the women go, and we can settle this man to man."

The killer paused. Meg held her breath. Then the killer giggled. The hood pulled back.

She stared in horror at the Raincoat Killer's face.

It was Rachel.

TWENTY-ONE

The sound of Rachel's laughter sent shivers down Jack's spine as the final piece of the puzzle he'd been pursuing for so long finally fell into crystal-clear focus.

"Rachel," Meg gasped. "What are you doing? Whatever Duncan or Wesley has told you, whatever they're making you do—" Her voice was lost to the clap of a thunder roar.

The jacket fell open, showing the pure white wedding dress on underneath. The smolder of disdain in Rachel's eyes had blazed into a full, raging anger. But the dancer's fingers stayed calm and steady on the trigger.

Oh, Lord, what should I say? What can I do?

"Rachel," Jack said, "where's Wesley?"

Lightning forked through the air. Jack counted silently under his breath. Before he could hit four seconds, thunder rolled again.

"Wesley and Duncan, Wesley and Duncan,"

Rachel snapped. "Is that all you can say? I told Meg. I don't know where Wesley is."

The boat swayed beneath them, but Rachel's footing stayed firm. *Balance of a dancer. Strength of an athlete. Mind of a killer.* "Do you really think either Duncan or Wesley is smart enough to be the mastermind behind any of this? Let alone strong enough to make me do anything I don't want to do."

Focus, Jack. Think like a journalist, and not like a hostage. What do you see? Her wedding dress was full and knee-length, so he couldn't count on it harming her agility. Her knuckles were pale. Her voice shook. Okay, so she was frustrated. This was a woman with a plan. A well-thought-out plan—he suspected—and he'd just thrown a wrench into it. And now she was stalling while she tried to figure out what to do.

Meg stepped back. "I don't understand."

"I do," Jack said, his hands raised, his voice steady. "Rachel, I'm sorry for not seeing it sooner. Wesley was vulnerable. Duncan was volatile and violent. But you, Rachel, were the cunning one. You were the brains behind this entire hoax."

"Hoax?" Rachel spluttered. "Is that all you think this is? This was about setting things right. Did you know Krista Hooper was a third-rate dancer who didn't deserve half the callbacks she got, let alone any of the parts she landed? Do you have any idea how hard it was for me to sit there, time and time again, and watch her get the roles that I deserved?

"With Wesley moving to England, I had to get that London audition. There was no way I was going to let Krista Hooper take it away from me. So I broke into her room, just looking for something to discredit her. But then she came home early. She called me 'a delusional, entitled diva.'"

A snarl turned the corner of her lips.

A shiver ran down Jack's spine. "So you hit her with a lamp."

"It was self-defense. She should have just admitted she cheated."

Images of the crime scene flashed like a slide show through his mind. There was no sign Krista even had a chance to fight back. *No, Jack. Don't get sidetracked. You need to get out alive. You need to get Meg out alive. You've got to find a way to distract her so you can get the gun away from her. Interview her. Do your job. You've interviewed plenty of criminals before.*

"How did Duncan get involved in this?" he asked.

"I called him after Krista died. He's been caught up in stuff before and I knew he'd understand. Besides, I ended up needing him to do something for me."

Jack felt Meg's hand brush against his side.

Everything inside him wanted to take her into his arms and away from this tiny room, with the barrel of a gun to their faces and the ravings of the delusional bride blocking the door. "So you killed Eliza Penn for him?"

"Duncan was going to kill her anyway." Rachel sniffed. "He was furious with her for dumping him. It was my idea to be smart about it, and to do it when he had an alibi. It was my idea to make it look like the work of a serial killer too. Like the ferry schedules. It was supposed to be like a trail of bread crumbs, so that after everything was done, detectives could go, 'Oh, look, it was obviously a serial killer and it was all pointing to Manitoulin Island all along.' But they were only supposed to figure it out after it was all over." She shot Jack a withering glance. "Seriously, dude. I never imagined some reporter would jump the gun like you did. Does that mean you're smarter than the average cop or a lot more gullible?"

She was baiting him. He wasn't about to rise to it. "Why the island? What do you mean by after it was all over?"

Rachel's eyes rolled. Okay, so she wasn't about to answer that.

He tried again. "Why did you want Duncan to kill Shelly Day?"

The darkness crossed her eyes again. "I didn't. I never even met her. Duncan just saw her outside some bar one night and she insulted him. So he followed her home to talk some sense into her. One thing led to another and somehow she ended up dead. I don't know. I'm just glad he remembered about the raincoat and the flyers. Duncan's got a temper problem. Especially when he's insulted. He's taken too many drugs and they've scrambled his brain." Frustration rumbled through her timbre of the voice. "It wasn't part of the plan. I don't know what drugs he took before he boarded the ferry that made him decide to attack Meg for being 'rude' to him. He also wasn't supposed to kill some random old man, thinking he was related to the Duffs. Thankfully I made him go back and get the stupid note he tried to leave.

"But then he hires some kid he bought drugs off of to run around in a raincoat after he found out you were digging into things, and my rehearsal dinner was ruined! Along with my pavilion! Was he kidding me with that nonsense?"

Lightning flashed. Jack counted under his breath. Three seconds later, thunder rolled.

"It's your grandmother's pavilion." Meg's voice was soft but strong. "Why do you care about it so much? All this time, you were so insistent that's where your reception had to be. You had to get married here on the island, with a big, shiny celebration at the pavilion that practically everyone on the island was invited to, all for your grandmother, a woman you clearly don't like, despite the fact that she gave you everything you ever wanted."

"Everything I ever wanted?" Rachel barked out a laugh. "You think I didn't want a father in my life? You think I wanted to spend the first twelve years of my life living in the back of a car? Shuttling around from dirty motel room to dingy basement apartment while Mother cried and begged Grandma for money?"

"Your mother was a drug addict," Meg said. "Your grandmother begged her to come home and get help. Your father abandoned you."

"My father had no choice!" Rachel's voice rose to a scream. "He didn't want to leave me. My grandmother drove them apart and practically forced him to go by making us broke. Then she sentenced my mother to death and forced me to come live on this wretched island. You know she nearly didn't agree to pay for my university when I was accepted at Toronto? Then when she heard I was moving to London with Wesley, she threatened to cut me off financially again. She was too afraid we'd just elope or live together. She wanted us to have the big, shiny wedding my mother never had. What's next? My grandmother won't be happy until I give up every single one of my dreams and move back here to live the life she's chosen for me. So now she's going to die and take her beloved town with her."

"How?" Jack said. Just one word, one final question, which echoed through the cabin like an anchor.

Rachel grinned. "I planted an explosive device in the flower fountain. Duncan was supposed to die at the wedding reception tonight, along with everyone else. All my carefully planted bread crumbs would point to him being the Raincoat Killer. The police would think he tried to kill me at my own wedding. Wesley and I were supposed to be on the boat when it went off.

"The explosion should still be big enough to take out Grandma's retirement home, the whole of downtown and everyone in it, even if the rain keeps it from setting fire to the forest and spreading across the entire island. Then her money will be mine, and I'll finally be free."

Meg sucked in a painful breath that sounded more like a whimper. He could only imagine what must be going through her heart and mind.

"Let Meg go," he said. "You've got me. You've got revenge on your grandmother. But Meg's innocent, and she's been nothing but kind and caring to you and Wesley."

"Innocent? Her brother ruined Wesley's life!"

The storm broke fully, unleashing a downpour onto the decks, filling the small cabin with the sound of the rain. Water ran through the open window. The boat rocked as waves roiled around them.

"You know Wesley practically clung to me the first few months we were together? His parents were dead, and now he was the exact same age his cousin was when he died. It was all he could talk about. His cousin died at eighteen, so he felt like he should be dead too. He had nightmares about it. I couldn't live with that.

"I'm going to make it right. Benji killed Wesley's cousin. Therefore, Benji will die—and lose his sister too. That's why I needed you as my wedding planner. I needed to know you'd be in the middle of town when the bomb exploded so you would die, along with this wretched place. Then when you canceled on me, I had no choice but to bring you out here onto the boat to make sure you didn't survive. My Wesley deserves nothing less. Then I'll find him, he'll understand and we'll be happy again."

TWENTY-TWO

Meg followed Jack into the galley, single file. Rachel kept the gun trained on their faces. The room was narrow but deep. As dangerous as it was to fire buckshot indoors, if they could knock the gun from her hands just enough to get her to fire away from them, there was a chance the shot would get absorbed by the cabinets with little of it ricocheting back toward them.

"Wesley left you, Rachel," Meg said. "I know you love him. I know you want him. But killing me and destroying the town won't bring him back."

"Wesley loves me." Rachel's gun was trained on her face. "He only left because he couldn't handle being back here. I never should have let him talk to your brother yesterday. You know Benji actually had him believing he hadn't killed Chris? Once the island is gone, and you are gone, I will find him and set the record straight, and then he'll love me again. I will get him back. He belongs with me." She waved the gun toward Jack. Meg felt her heart pounding so hard in her chest she thought the world was going to spin out from underneath her.

Then she heard Jack's steady voice in her ear as he moved behind her. "It's okay, Meg. Breathe."

She gulped a cleansing breath and glanced at his face. But he was staring at his feet with his eyes almost completely closed. His lips moved, as if he was counting down to something.

"Move," Rachel barked.

Lightning forked outside the window, illuminating the sky and filling the tiny cabin. Spots danced before Meg's eyes, temporarily blinding her, before leaving behind a forked afterimage of light. Rachel hesitated.

"Meg! Run!" Jack threw himself at Rachel's legs and knocked her to the floor.

The sound of thunder filled the cabin, mingled with Rachel's screams of fury. Meg ran for the stairs up to the deck. Buckshot exploded in the galley behind her, shattering glass and splintering cabinets. Her fingers fumbled for the walkie-talkie as her feet reached the top of the stairs. She shoved open the hatch and felt the rush of heavy rain.

"Benji!" she shouted, clutching the walkie-talkie to her lips.

"Sis!" his voice crackled back. "Are you okay?"

"No. Rachel's the other killer. She might have shot Jack."

"I'm coming for you—" His engine roared.

"No. Don't! Go back to the island. Keep trying to call the police. There's a bomb in the pavilion. In the fountain of flowers. They have to evacuate the town before it goes off."

Static greeted her on the other end.

Then he said, "But what about you?"

"I'll be okay. I've got Jack. I love you. Go—"

The blow of a sudden fist flew across her face, knocking her head sideways with such force her neck screamed in pain. The walkie-talkie fell from her hand. It slid across the deck and landed in the water beyond.

Dark clouds filled the skies. A thin figure in a black raincoat stood over her. Water poured down his body and pounded onto the deck. "What are you doing here?"

His hood fell back.

It was Detective Ravine.

"Detective! Please! We're in danger. There's a woman below with a gun. She's trying to kill Jack—you have to save him!"

His cold, dead eyes barely glanced at her face. His hand grabbed the hair at the base of her neck and forced her to her knees. Pain filled her skull as the detective's unrelenting grip forced her down to her knees.

Was this why Toronto's chief of police thought Jack was crazy? Was one of his own detectives misleading the police department and helping the Raincoat Killer?

Oh, Lord, help Benji navigate safely through the waves. Help him reach the police in time. Save Jack. Save me.

"How did you get here?" Detective Ravine shouted over the roar. "Who else is here? Who were you just talking to? Where is Rachel?"

"I'm here, Dad." Rachel's head appeared through the hatch.

Dad? Meg glanced from the bride's wide, wild eyes up to the wiry detective who now held her in his grasp.

Detective Ravine was Rachel's father? The man who'd abandoned his daughter all those years ago had returned for her wedding after all.

Rachel climbed onto the deck, her motions unusually stilted, jerky, like a puppet on a string. Then Meg saw Jack coming through the hatch behind her. With one strong hand Jack grasped the back of Rachel's neck like a truant kitten's. The killer bride fell onto her hands and knees on the waterlogged deck. Her eyes were level with Meg's. The two women knelt face-to-face.

Ravine looked down at his daughter. "What did you do?" he snapped. "You brought them on board? I told you to forget about her!"

His daughter's eyes looked up into his. Tears and rain streamed down her cheeks as she tried to explain. "But she had to die. For what her brother did to Wesley. She wasn't going to be in the pavilion anymore and I couldn't risk her getting away. She had to see the bomb explode."

Ravine looked away. His eyes cut to the journalist standing on the deck across from him. "What do you want?"

"I want you to free Meg," Jack said. "Let her off this boat safely and we'll let you and your daughter go."

A smirk twisted at the corner of Ravine's mouth. His eyes grew cold with a depth of darkness that threatened to paralyze Meg's heart in her chest. "You think I'm about to barter anything for that little rat's life?" He barked out a laugh. "Just do me a favor and try not to hurt her until the evil old bat of her grandmother explodes in a ball of flames first. Then you can do whatever you want to my little golden goose."

Ravine crouched down, until his face was level with hers. "You see, sweetie, the moment I stumbled upon the shambled mess you made of the Krista Hooper crime scene, ran a DNA test on the blood you'd left on the carpet and discovered my long-lost baby girl was behind it, I knew my ship had finally come in. To think, my baby was back and was a foolish, ruthless killer, no less, who I could use to get exactly what I want. All I had to do was watch you and your addict friend Duncan commit your stupid little murders while I stayed in the shadows and helped you cover your tracks, while making sure I'd be in the position to inherit when you finally went too far. If only you could have seen the look on your face when I knocked on your door, to introduce myself as your long-lost papa. It was so easy to plant the idea in your head that it was time we both went after the real villain, the one who robbed us both of what we so clearly deserved, your grandmother."

Rachel's head shook. A sob escaped her lips. "But I'm your daughter. We're in this together. I just found you again."

Ravine leaned in until his face was inches away from hers. "Pathetic that you never thought to question how I threw you and your mother away to begin with." He glanced to Jack. "Go ahead. Drown her. I really don't care. Saves me having to do it myself. I already scared off her beloved Wesley this morning."

Jack let go of Rachel. He leapt back as Rachel threw herself on Ravine, crashing into him with such a force it knocked them both to the floor. Ravine's grasp fell from Meg. He raised both hands to his face in defense as his daughter furiously scratched and clawed at the man who had betrayed her. Jack pulled Meg tightly into his side, wrapping his arm around his shoulder.

Meg clung to Jack, burying her face in his chest.

"How did you know that if you let her go, she'd attack him and not you?"

"Hunch." He kissed her head. Then he pressed the pocketknife into her hand. "Now we've got to stop them before they kill each other. They're not getting off that easy. They deserve to face justice for what they did."

Ravine had Rachel down on the deck now. For all her fury, he was more than her match in size and strength. His hands tightened around her throat. Rachel screamed in anger and terror. Jack grabbed the detective around the neck and yanked him off her. Rachel leapt to her knees. But in an instant, the killer bride froze as she felt the warning prick of Meg's blade at the back of her neck.

"Hands behind your head," Meg said. Rachel complied.

Jack hauled Ravine to his feet, the detective struggling helplessly against his choke hold. "You made a pledge to protect the innocent and uphold justice. Not to mention the obligation any decent man would feel to care for the daughter you made. You disgust me." Jack's eyes met Meg's. "I'm going to lock him in a cupboard belowdecks until the police can get here and arrest them both. Give me a two-minute head start and then bring her down. Okay?"

She nodded. "Can you hand me the end of that tow rope?" Jack frog-marched Ravine to the railing, then unhooked the rope from the life buoy and passed it to her. Meg wrapped it, one-handed, around Rachel's wrists, pulling it tight with her teeth, while her other hand held the knife firm to Rachel's neck. It wasn't much of a knot, but it was enough to keep Rachel from fighting back.

"Impressive," Jack said.

"Blame Benji. No one ties a tarp down one-handed in a storm like him." She looked out over the storm.

"Your brother made it safely, Meg," Jack said, as if reading her thoughts.

"I know." She'd known it the moment she'd asked him to turn his boat around and drive through a storm toward an impending explosion. That aching, paralyzing fear for his safely had left her. Her brother could handle it, and she'd been wrong to treat him like a kid as long as she had.

"I'll be back in one second." Jack pushed Ravine belowdecks.

Meg sat back on her heels. One hand clenched the rope around Rachel's hands. The other kept the knife still.

Rachel was sobbing now, but Meg couldn't tell if the tears rolling down her cheeks were real or fake.

"I really thought he cared about me," Rachel whimpered. "But no one does. Not my father. Not

Wesley. Nobody loves me. And all I ever did was love them."

Pity filled Meg's heart, but when she spoke her voice had a strength that seemed to come from somewhere far deeper and stronger. "No, you didn't. You grabbed on to them because you wanted *them* to love *you*. You want to know what real love actually is? Look at your grandmother. She loves you. I cared about you too, Rachel. Jack just saved your life, even though you hardly deserve it. And I'm going to pray you learn, someday, to accept that kind of love, God's love, real love, and that you'll finally learn to love someone else in return."

Rachel snarled, "What could you possibly know about love?"

"Ready?" Jack's appeared back through the hatch. Water streaming down the lines of his face. His cheek was scratched and a deep bruise had formed at the edge of his temple. She could only imagine how tired and sore he must be feeling. Her heart filled with emotions she could hardly put words to—warmth, affection, respect, awe.

"More than you'll ever know," Meg said. Enough to know she needed to let him go, let him be the wild, free, courageous, risk-taking man that he needed to be, without her and her fears holding him back. "Now get up." She stood slowly, pulling Rachel up to her feet.

Lightning filled the sky again. Thunder rolled around them. Rachel kicked backward like a mule, catching Meg hard just below the knee. Meg fell back, dropping the knife and letting go of Rachel. Her shoes slid on the slick, water-soaked deck. The railing smacked against her calves. Her feet lost their grip. For a moment, the clouds above filled her view as she flew overboard.

Meg's body hit the water.

TWENTY-THREE

She was tumbling underwater. Darkness filled her eyes as her body was tossed by the undertow. She couldn't see the light on any side. There was no way to know which direction was up. The storm had churned the muddy ground, filling the water with stones and sand. Grit stung her eyes. Then she saw a figure beside her in the water and felt his strong arm around her waist, directing her toward the surface. She kicked hard. They broke through the water. She gasped as fresh rain poured over her face again.

"You okay?" Jack treaded water beside her. His arm held her fast.

"Always." She smiled. "Thank you."

"Any time."

They swam to shore, side by side, battling the waves that threatened to send them back underwater. Their feet stumbled over the rocky shore. Finally Jack reached a young pine tree, growing out over the water's edge. Grabbing the narrow trunk with one hand, he pulled her to it, waited until she dragged herself to shore and then climbed up after her. He dropped to the ground. She curled up beside him and bowed her head against his as they thanked God for their survival.

Then she opened her eyes. Ahead of them, the yacht danced like a cork on the water. "What happened to Rachel and her father?"

"I forced her back through the hatch and tied her hands to the doorknob. Her father is locked in the cupboard. He can't get anywhere near her. Though to be fair, she has enough rage in her right now to do him some serious damage if she can get past his defenses, especially if he was telling the truth about scaring off her fiancé in order to claim her inheritance for himself. Last I heard they were screaming abuse at each other. Once the police arrive they'll probably race to see who can turn the other one in first. It's sad. They have no idea how alike they really are." He pointed to the bright light of a police rescue boat cutting through the water toward them. "Looks like they won't have that long to wait."

She leaned into his side, soaking in his warmth as his arm took its place over her shoulders. "You saved the Raincoat Killer's life. I can't imagine how big a scoop that will be."

He chuckled. "Technically there were three Raincoat Killers—Rachel, Detective Ravine and Duncan." He sighed. "I just wish I'd put the clues together earlier. Maybe I could've prevented McCarthy's death and stopped Stuart from being shot—"

She slid a gentle finger over his mouth. "No what-ifs. Not anymore. What did you tell me about second-guessing God?"

He smiled. He pulled her finger away from his lips, kissed it gently and then tucked her hand into his.

"I'm sorry, Jack." Sudden tears slipped from her eyes.

He dropped her hand and cupped her face in both of his. "Whatever for?"

"I wanted you to give this up. Your job. Chasing down stories like this. To sit behind a desk and not take risks, just like I wanted Benji to stay my baby brother forever. But you were the only one who realized the truth about the Raincoat Killer, and if you hadn't pressed your editor to run the story and followed your instincts..." Her voice trailed off.

"If I hadn't," he said, his voice gentle, "God would have sent someone else to do the job. If I quit the story today, some other reporter will take it up."

She looked into his eyes. "But that's the point. I don't want God to send somebody else. I want Him to send you. I want you to be out there, listening to your gut, tracking down killers and helping victims feel safe and listened to, no matter where that takes you. Because that's who you are. That's who you need to be. I never should have asked you to give that up, not for anything, not for me.

"That's why you have to go back to Toronto and write the story of how you unmasked the Raincoat Killers and stopped them. You need to stay on this story and cover the trials until everyone is brought to justice. For their victims, for the public, for me, as only you can do it. If that means you need to walk away from me, for however long it takes, because being with me is going to get in the way of you reporting on this story, then I want you to do it. No one else on the planet knows this story like you do. If you hand it off to some new reporter, then the true story might never get told."

He groaned. Then his lips brushed over her hair. "But it will definitely be months." His breath hovered over her face. "Maybe even years, of seeing each other's name in the news, of seeing each other across crowded courtrooms, of writing about you but not being able to be with you."

She looked down. "I know. But you have to do this, Jack. You have to finish what you started."

Dark warmth pooled in his eyes, sending shivers cascading through her limbs, pouring into her heart. Then he raised her face to his and gently kissed her goodbye.

* * *

Late-afternoon sun beat down on Meg's limbs. She sat on top of the picnic table, wrapped her arms around her knees and watched as a beaming groom led his beautiful bride down the boardwalk to the pavilion. They waved to Meg as they passed. She waved back. It had been a week since the explosive device Rachel had planted in the pavilion forced the town's emergency evacuation.

Now Rachel, Duncan and the disgraced Detective Ravine were behind bars awaiting trial while the police reopened every murder investigation from the beginning. Stuart was out of the hospital and on the mend. Kenny had taken a plea bargain and would spend just six weeks in jail. And Wesley had been found, alive and well, in Ottawa. She prayed they would all get the help and healing they needed.

Meanwhile, Alyssa Burne had kindly agreed to take over all of Meg's weddings for the next six weeks. Her town and her community would understand. Meg needed a vacation. She needed rest.

"Hey, sis!" Benji strode up the beach. A newspaper was wedged under his arm. "Have you heard about this?" He held the paper up for her to see. There was a mug shot of Rachel on the front cover, bedraggled from the rain with an orange raincoat hanging open over a tattered wedding dress. The headline read Face-to-Face with the Raincoat Killers—by Jack Brooks.

Meg shook her head. "No. And I don't need to read it. I remember it all just fine, thank you very much." She hadn't spoken to Jack since she stepped onto the police rescue boat, into the welcoming hug from her brother, and heard the news that the bomb had been stopped. She'd felt Jack's eyes on her the whole ride back, but their goodbyes had already been said. As the boat reached shore, she'd left with her brother. Jack had stayed with the police as Ravine and Rachel were arrested.

From there, Jack had gone back to Toronto to sit through police briefings and meetings with his team, gather his notes and write pages upon pages of words that would be printed and reprinted in newspapers across the world. Already, news outlets were announcing he'd received a formal apology from the Toronto police, not to mention signed a major book deal.

She knew Benji was surprised, maybe even annoyed, that Jack hadn't called. But she wasn't. She knew she had to let him go. Not out of fear, but out of respect for the man he was and the man he needed to be. He needed the professional distance to write the best story he could, to get that book deal and to be syndicated, without any professional complications, accusations of bias or the raised eyebrows that might come from the star reporter being involved with a victim of the killers' crimes.

He couldn't ask her to wait for him while the case wound its way through the courts. She couldn't ask him to jeopardize the huge opportunities that lay ahead of him now with the professional risk that a romantic entanglement with her would be.

"I think you should read this." Benji opened the paper to the third page and laid it flat on the top of the table beside her.

She tossed her head. "I really don't need to."

"Sis." His voice was firm, with an unexpected authority that brought a smile to her cheeks. "Trust me. Read this." His finger pointed to a bold box of text, nestled at the bottom of the article. "In fact, read it out loud."

"Okay. Fine.... 'Declaration of Personal Bias by Jack Brooks,'" she said. "'While investigating the so-called Raincoat Killers on Manitoulin Island, I stayed in the home of one of the killers' attempted victims, wedding organizer Meg Duff and her brother, Benjamin. I grew to like and respect them both very much and consider them friends.

"'Now, there's a rule in my line of work that reporters should never get too close to the subject of a story, or else they risk blurring the lines between reporter and interviewee. As many of my faithful readers know, I have been following the story of the Raincoat Killers since it first broke almost four months ago. I intend to follow this story through to the end, investigate every lead, follow every thread and hold both the accused and law enforcement to account, with integrity, honesty and the utmost of professionalism, until those responsible for the deaths and assaults attributed to the Raincoat Killers are behind bars.

"'However, my medium is truth, and my oath as a journalist is to speak the truth, wherever I find it, no matter how inconvenient to some—including myself. The truth of the matter is that Meg Duff is the most courageous, beautiful, exquisite... '"

The words faded as her breath caught in her throat, stealing the air from her lungs.

"Exquisite creature I've ever had the privilege of meeting," said a strong, warm, familiar voice behind her. She turned. Jack was standing behind her, and her brother was already halfway down the beach.

"And I have fallen quite deeply in love with her." A smile twinkled in the depths of his eyes. He stepped forward, until the strength of his chest brushed up against hers. "So I have asked the paper's publisher, my team and our syndicators to grant me permission to pursue a relationship with her, openly and honestly. Because whether she is standing right by my side throughout the coming months," he recited, "or somewhere as far off as 'professional distance' demands—" his breath tickled over her skin "—she will always and forever be first on my mind and in my heart, as close to me as the air that I breathe."

She smiled. "You actually wrote and published that?"

"I actually did." His fingers slid into the hair and brushed along the back of her neck. "It was the most honest thing I've ever written. For a moment there, it looked like I was going to lose my job over it. It took some careful planning, a lot of meetings with my publisher and Vince really going to bat for me, to convince *Torchlight News* they couldn't afford to just let their star reporter go in the middle of the biggest story of his career. But it had to be done. I love you, Meg, and I can't pretend otherwise a moment longer."

She reached for him, her body aching for the feel of his arms. But instead of pulling her into the hug that she longed for, he pulled away.

His dark eyes looked so deeply into hers she felt shivers down her spine. "But I've got to be honest with you, Meg. If you decide to take this journey with me, it's not going to be easy. These trials could last years. Meanwhile, court television shows and gossip mongers are going to have a field day over the idea of a crime reporter and a survivor being together romantically. Our testimonies will both be under extra scrutiny during the trial. The tabloid reporters will be knocking at your door. If this leads to marriage, the international news will go wild. Paparazzi around the globe will be coming after you."

"Then let them come." She stood up on the picnic bench and looped her arms around his neck. "I love you, Jack, and as long as we're together, I'm not scared."

Then his mouth moved over hers, and he kissed her with a passion that stole the breath from her lungs and quelled every last whisper of doubt in her heart.

* * * * *

Dear Reader,

Thank you for sharing Meg and Jack's story with me. While the specific locations, buildings and people in this book are a work of fiction, Manitoulin Island itself is far more interesting and culturally rich than I could possibly have words to describe. The ferry journey on a clear day is simply beautiful.

Like Meg, I've always battled anxiety. I remember, as a teenager, standing on a beach watching my friends leaping off a cliff into the water while fear held me back like a hand on my chest. I'm very grateful to God for all of the various people in my life who've been there for me, to listen, to guide or to just stand beside me. Especially my husband, who gives me both the wind for my sails and a safe harbor to come home to.

My prayer for you is that if there's anything in your life holding you back, you will find the people, the places and the support you need to adventure and grow into the beautiful person God calls you to be.

Please drop by and visit me online at www.maggiekblack.com. I really enjoy hearing your thoughts and am thankful that you are sharing this journey with me.

Maggie

Questions for Discussion

1. When Meg is on the ferry and starts to feel stressed, she heads out alone onto the foggy deck to find some peace. When you feel overwhelmed, do you prefer to be alone or with people?

2. Would you prefer joining a friend for a high-intensity activity like snowmobiling or a calmer one like hiking in the woods? Are there any adventure sports that you have tried or would like to try?

3. Why do you think the snowmobiling accident affected Benji and Meg so differently?

4. Are there ever times in which fear is a healthy thing that keeps us from making bad decisions? Are there times when fear holds us back from good things? How do we tell the difference?

5. What role can friends, family, health professionals and our church play in helping us overcome our fears and follow God's best for our life? What do you think will help Meg?

6. When Chris Quay died in a snowmobiling accident, his friends tied ribbons to a tree to

remember him. Fourteen years later, the ribbon tree is still there, and the small community still remembers his death. Does that surprise you? Have you ever seen a roadside memorial to a traffic accident?

7. When Jack first questions Meg about Benji, he is skeptical of the faith she has in her brother, because it reminds him of times he's heard criminals blindly defended by their family and friends. Do you think Meg is right to have faith in her brother? What causes us to have faith in other people?

8. What do you think of Meg's relationship with her brother, Benji? How do you think the events in this book will change her relationship with him?

9. Jack risked his career and reputation with his dogged determination to investigate the Raincoat Killer, even though the chief of police said there was no such serial killer. Did Jack do the right thing? Is there anything you think he should or could have done differently?

10. Meg is worried she can't have a future with Jack because of the risks he takes in his job and his love of dangerous sports. What advice would you have given Jack at the beginning of

the book, if he'd asked you how much of himself he should change in order to have a future
with Meg? How do you think being with Meg
will change him?

11. How do you think the story would have ended
    differently if Jack had written a story about
    Meg without her agreeing to be interviewed?

12. Do you enjoy hearing about criminal inves-
    tigations and murder trials in the news? Do
    you watch television news programs that fol-
    low trials and investigations currently taking
    place? Why or why not?

13. Is Meg right to think that if the news reported
    that the Raincoat Killer attacked her, some
    brides might think twice about using her as a
    wedding planner? Why or why not?

14. When Jack is attacked by someone in a rain-
    coat in the sports store, Meg decides to help
    him instead of running away. Why do you
    think she did that? What do you think of her
    decision?

15. Throughout the book Meg is determined that
    she doesn't want the media harassing her or
    prying into her personal life. Yet at the end of
    the book she makes the decision to be with

Jack, even though she knows it will probably result in the tabloids following her for a while. Why does she make that choice? Why do you think she's not afraid anymore?

LARGER-PRINT BOOKS!

GET 2 FREE
LARGER-PRINT NOVELS
PLUS 2 FREE
MYSTERY GIFTS

Love Inspired

Larger-print novels are now available...

YES! Please send me 2 FREE LARGER-PRINT Love Inspired® novels and my 2 FREE mystery gifts (gifts are worth about $10). After receiving them, if I don't wish to receive any more books, I can return the shipping statement marked "cancel." If I don't cancel, I will receive 6 brand-new novels every month and be billed just $5.24 per book in the U.S. or $5.74 per book in Canada. That's a savings of at least 23% off the cover price. It's quite a bargain! Shipping and handling is just 50¢ per book in the U.S. and 75¢ per book in Canada.* I understand that accepting the 2 free books and gifts places me under no obligation to buy anything. I can always return a shipment and cancel at any time. Even if I never buy another book, the two free books and gifts are mine to keep forever.

122/322 IDN F49Y

Name _____ (PLEASE PRINT) _____

Address _____ Apt. # _____

City _____ State/Prov. _____ Zip/Postal Code _____

Signature (if under 18, a parent or guardian must sign) _____

Mail to the Harlequin® Reader Service:
IN U.S.A.: P.O. Box 1867, Buffalo, NY 14240-1867
IN CANADA: P.O. Box 609, Fort Erie, Ontario L2A 5X3

Are you a current subscriber to Love Inspired books
and want to receive the larger-print edition?
Call 1-800-873-8635 or visit www.ReaderService.com.

* Terms and prices subject to change without notice. Prices do not include applicable taxes. Sales tax applicable in N.Y. Canadian residents will be charged applicable taxes. Offer not valid in Quebec. This offer is limited to one order per household. Not valid for current subscribers to Love Inspired Larger-Print books. All orders subject to credit approval. Credit or debit balances in a customer's account(s) may be offset by any other outstanding balance owed by or to the customer. Please allow 4 to 6 weeks for delivery. Offer available while quantities last.

Your Privacy—The Harlequin® Reader Service is committed to protecting your privacy. Our Privacy Policy is available online at www.ReaderService.com or upon request from the Harlequin Reader Service.

We make a portion of our mailing list available to reputable third parties that offer products we believe may interest you. If you prefer that we not exchange your name with third parties, or if you wish to clarify or modify your communication preferences, please visit us at www.ReaderService.com/consumerschoice or write to us at Harlequin Reader Service Preference Service, P.O. Box 9062, Buffalo, NY 14269. Include your complete name and address.

LILPDIR13R

ReaderService.com

Manage your account online!

- Review your order history
- Manage your payments
- Update your address

---

*We've designed
the Harlequin® Reader Service
website just for you.*

Enjoy all the features!

- Reader excerpts from any series
- Respond to mailings and
  special monthly offers
- Discover new series available to you
- Browse the Bonus Bucks catalog
- Share your feedback

Visit us at:
ReaderService.com